ELIZA HOPE-BROWN

Colours

Two souls intertwined across time
Always destined to find each other
No matter what it takes
Or the consequences

Even in their darkest moments
They're fated to find each other
Like pieces of a beautiful cosmic puzzle
That always find a way to click into place

One of them always knowing
Understanding the sweet inevitability
Particles of the stars once blown apart
Always finding their way home

~ EHB

Contents

Foreword	iii
Acknowledgement	iv
Chapter 1	1
Chapter 2	8
Chapter 3	16
Chapter 4	24
Chapter 5	34
Chapter 6	44
Chapter 7	51
Chapter 8	56
Chapter 9	61
Chapter 10	72
Chapter 11	78
Chapter 12	87
Chapter 13	95
Chapter 14	105
Chapter 15	112
Chapter 16	119
Chapter 17	128
Chapter 18	135
Chapter 19	142
Chapter 20	152
Chapter 21	160
Chapter 22	166

Chapter 23   173

Chapter 24   180

Chapter 25   189

Chapter 26   196

Chapter 27   204

Chapter 28   209

Chapter 29   217

Chapter 30   223

Chapter 31   228

Chapter 32   237

Chapter 33   245

Chapter 34   254

Chapter 35   261

Epilogue   270

About the Author   272

Also by Eliza Hope-Brown   273

Foreword

Sweet Inevitably Series

Different universes. Different timelines. Different iterations of the same people.

Can Dan and Laura find their matching pieces in every world?

The same hearts, different lives. Will love find a way?

Books in this series:

Sanctuary

Colours

Acknowledgement

As I draw my second story to a close, I never thought I'd be writing more acknowledgements.

Undoubtedly, I have to thank all the readers of Sanctuary who loved that story, and who encouraged me to tell another version of this love story. Every sale, review and positive comment from my first book has inspired me to write this one, so thank you.

To my test readers, Gee and Julie, whose time and insights in the process have been invaluable, thank you so much for giving up your time to read this story and help me shape it in the way I have done.

And finally, no acknowledgement would be complete without me thanking Daisy who is the keystone of all my work. Her heart is woven through every line in this book. She is more than a friend and an editor, she is a fierce protector of me and my work and has had such a huge input into how this story has been told. Not every writing session together is easy and even when the hard conversations have been needed, she has been there for me.

The Playlist

I have always been a lover of music from a very young age. As cliched as it sounds, music is regularly the soundtrack to my life and you'll often find me plugged into something listening to my favourite songs.

Large portions of this story you're about to read were written to specific songs that I listened to on repeat.

I have collected them into a single randomised Spotify playlist for you to listen to and enjoy while you read.

Enjoy!

Chapter 1

The Kiss

"Devastated!" She said, full of mirth and Prosecco. "No one to kiss at midnight."

As Dan shared her laughter at her predicament, he realised how much she'd changed since he'd seen her in the summer. Three months before, she'd left for university a girl but she'd come back a woman. It wasn't so much a physical change but one that was more deeply rooted in her growing confidence as a person. Gone was the slight awkwardness and unfamiliarity of body, and what had replaced it was a gorgeous woman who could probably very easily convince him to do things he really shouldn't do, even though he was essentially like her big brother. He studied her as she leaned against the doorframe in her beautiful black dress. It seemed to have a divine way of hugging her thick curves in all the right places, with its bewitching plunging neckline, and he had to inwardly admit that she did, in fact, look hot.

He tried to shake the fuzzy feelings of confusion out of his head. "Sorry kid, can't help you."

"Hey! You don't get to call me that anymore," she laughed,

"I'm all grown up now."

"So I can see," he said looking at her, trying to keep his eyes above her chin.

*

The Muir family had been friends with the Gray family for longer than Laura Gray and Dan Muir had been alive. Their parents had met thirty five years before while on a couples' holiday in the Mediterranean. Not *that* kind of couples' holiday, but one where they'd ended up talking over dinner one evening at the hotel restaurant, after three consecutive nights sitting at adjacent tables, not so much as saying hello. The friendship, however, would last a lifetime and would intertwine the two growing families for its duration, in ways no one could have fully anticipated in the beginning.

Isobel, fondly known by those close to her as Issy, was born first to Brian and Molly Muir, followed by a sweet boy called Daniel, two years later. Emily and Dave Gray were delighted when asked to be godparents to both the Muir children and over the ensuing years, the Grays became like second parents to Issy and Dan.

Back in those days, things like IVF weren't commonplace and for a time, the Grays struggled to conceive, no matter how much or how often they tried. Seeing Issy and Dan grow up to be such great kids, just made them want that life for themselves. And then after a *lot* of trying, ten years after shy, little Dan Muir arrived on the scene, Emily found out she was pregnant with what would be their only child. Laura, much wanted and very loved, was born a few months later.

The children all grew up together, such was the way of the

two families. Not content spending weekends and holidays with each other, year in and year out, they would hang out after school, a scandal of shoes adorning the front steps of both homes on a daily basis.

They spent so much time together, the three children, that Dan, being ten years older, took Laura under his wing as his adopted baby sister. As the years turned into a decade, Dan had been little Laura's closest friend, protector and shoulder to cry on. He had scared off many a stupid boy who wanted to mess with his Laura while being her biggest supporter in all her endeavours, even when they were misguided. Like the time she tried to sing karaoke at his 21st birthday party when she was only eleven. She'd hit every note wrong and had not been in time once but Dan had cheered her on like she was in the Pop Idol final.

When she got into university aged eighteen, Dan had been on the phone to congratulate her within the hour and spent the whole evening in the pub, telling everyone who would listen that Laura had got into her first choice uni. That night, so exuberant were his celebrations, he couldn't even remember getting home.

As a token of his affection for her, Dan had bought her a little silver locket as a going-away present and placed photos of each of them inside. Dan on the left, Laura on the right.

"Something so you can carry us with you anywhere you go, we will always be together and it's yours forever, no matter what," he'd told her.

She'd fallen in love with it from the moment she opened the box and it had sat around her neck ever since. It was a little piece of him that she kept with her always and he was glad she did. But now she was back and clearly in the mood

3

to celebrate herself.

*

"Sorry kid, can't help you."

"Hey! You don't get to call me that any more," she laughed, "I'm all grown up now."

"So I can see," he said looking at her, trying to keep his eyes above her chin.

Laura's pout was the same as it ever was though, regardless of her age. "Seriously Dan! It's not funny. Who am I meant to kiss at midnight?"

He couldn't help but laugh. "Hey, I'm in no position to give advice on the issue! You must have noticed that I turned up alone tonight. I won't be kissing anyone when midnight strikes; I'll just be sipping whiskey and coke."

"Then we'll have to kiss each other!" The alcohol was giving her a much-needed confidence boost. He might have been one of her oldest friends in the world and for the most part, the big brother she never had; but arriving back from uni more sure of herself, Laura had been greeted by a feast to the eyes when Dan had walked in earlier that evening. He was ten years older, sure, but looking at him over the top of her Prosecco glass, wearing a pair of fitted blue jeans and a thick black winter jumper, he looked good. Really, really good. Deep down inside, there was so much she wanted, but Laura hadn't even kissed a guy properly, let alone done anything more serious.

"I'm not sure kissing your nose like I used to when you were crying as a kid is what New Year's is all about." He was playing with fire and knew it but she wasn't a kid anymore so he felt like a bit of flirty teasing wouldn't do any harm.

"Two minutes till midnight!" Emily shouted from the living room.

Laura smirked as she slowly closed the distance between her and Dan, holding his gaze like a big cat stalking helpless prey. "So then don't kiss my nose."

When she stopped in front of him, Dan realised he was trembling and in fucking trouble. "That wouldn't be a sensible idea would it?" He gave her a gentle *come on, don't be a prat* smile but couldn't avoid noticing how attractive she looked.

"Maybe Dan, but it's New Year's." Her eyelash extensions fluttered as she lowered her voice, licking her lips lasciviously.

"Still not a good idea…" Dan breathed, lowering his own voice. She was so close he only needed to whisper. *Fuck Dan get out of this situation, now. She's basically your baby sister.*

"Thirty seconds everyone!" Laura's mum seemed to be acting as their own personal countdown without realising she was in control of a highly explosive situation. "Ten! Nine! Eight!"

Laura was closer to Dan than she had been in months. Her belly fizzed with excitement as an inner clock seemed to tick away deep inside her, uncontrollably.

"Seven! Six! Five!" Emily kept counting them down.

"Laura, we shouldn't…" He should have moved back, removed himself entirely from the fireworks about to explode in the Grays' kitchen. But he didn't.

"Four! Three! Two!"

And then her lips were on his. The shock nearly knocked him off his feet and would've done, had he not been leaning up against the kitchen counter. Dan's mind reeled as the cheers of *Happy New Year* rang through the house but he quickly became aware that he was kissing her too. This wasn't a one-sided kiss. His lips moved with hers for what felt like an eternity, a kiss as gentle as if it was her first. *Am I her first kiss?!* He had to stop this. It wasn't right. He knew it, even if her drunk ass didn't. The way her lips tasted like strawberries though, he knew that taste would forever be his favourite, from this breath till his last.

The next thing Dan knew, he was holding her at arm's length by the shoulders shaking his head clear; both of them breathing hard. "Laura stop!" He tried to slow his breathing and gain some vague sense of control. "We can't. You know I love you like my baby sister but you need to try kissing someone closer to your own age right now. That's what uni is for. Finding yourself and what you want. And who."

Looking away from him but not moving, Laura scrunched up her nose, the sure sign of awkwardness he'd seen her do her whole life. "Sorry. I just…I dunno. Sorry." Guilt washed over her, yet it wasn't accompanied by regret and she didn't understand why.

"Hey, you have nothing to be sorry for, these things happen, kid. Let's just draw a line under it and move on okay? I'm not mad. I just don't think us two kissing is a good idea, that's all." *This is my sister!*

She knew he was right. He often was when it came to matters of the heart and it was annoying, for the most part.

"Happy New Year," Dan said, pulling her into a hug and affectionately kissing her forehead.

Laura wrapped her arms around his chest and clung on, grateful that he was in her life. Her lips still tasted of him, and she liked it. "So I can go kiss boys at uni now?" She asked playfully.

"Ah well, no. You could, but between me and your dad, they'd not live long." He was only half joking and they both knew it.

She smiled and hugged him tight, the familiar scent of his sandalwood aftershave getting tangled in her blonde hair. She loved that smell. "Thanks, Dan. Love you."

"Love you too," he replied, holding her as the new year began.

Buddy, their Border Collie puppy scampered into the kitchen and bumped his wet nose onto Dan's calf.

"Yes Buddy, we love you too."

Chapter 2

The Other Guy

Twelve months later and another year was coming to a close. Dan stood in his parents' kitchen talking to his mum who was rotating mini sausage rolls on a large baking tray before putting them back in the oven to finish off.

"You looking forward to seeing Laura?" She asked.

"Yeah, I am. Don't get to spend much time together at all now she's at uni so it will be good to see her.

"Don't forget she's bringing her new boyfriend."

"Don't worry Mum, I'll be on my best behaviour, I promise. She says she's happy so that's all that matters to me."

"I didn't think you'd act up Dan, I was more concerned it might be odd for you to see her with someone else." Molly Muir washed her hands under the tap and dried them on her apron as she looked at her son.

"It's not that it'll be odd, Mum. She's never been my girlfriend. But as someone who cares for her a lot, I just want her to be happy. And you know what I'm like, I keep my circle close."

"Mhmm. Just play nicely please, you know what you and

8

Martin can be like when you get going, you might terrify the poor lad!"

*

Dan smiled, but couldn't help feeling the prickles of anxiety starting to build on his skin. Laura being away at university was a new dynamic for their friendship and it left them seeing much less of each other, having to make up the difference with regular catch-up phone calls. He knew from his own experience that uni could be tough and it was often the case that when he'd called, she'd been busy or stressed with coursework so their conversations had been short and concise. Ever the protector, he satisfied himself that he'd checked in and then left her to do what she needed to do, even though he missed her.

She'd told him about her new boyfriend earlier in the year, but to date had not yet brought him along to any family functions. In a way, Dan felt for him, about to be thrust into a staple family gathering for the first time but his focus was ensuring his adopted baby sister was happy. Anything else was additional. The boy needed to be weighed and measured.

Laura had spoken to Dan at length about Chris a few days before, on a Boxing Day walk with Buddy. He was in her year at university, although they took different classes. He even played football for the uni team and was apparently pretty good by all accounts, although Dan wasn't particularly interested or impressed by that, football wasn't much of a family thing for the Muirs; they were more a rugby bunch, with Dan having a particular love for the NFL. He noted how even though she spoke fondly of her new man, that she wasn't particularly gushing with love. Dan put it down to her being new to this kind of adult dating which you only really start to experience once you leave home.

As he'd dropped her back home he'd asked, "does he make you happy, kid?"

"I'm happy," she smiled at him.

"Then that's all that matters to me. I'm looking forward to meeting him next week."

Now he was to encounter the boyfriend for the first time and the protector in him was wanting to wander around with his chest puffed out and a baseball bat close to hand.

*

The latch turned in the front door and Laura's soft happy voice filtered through the house.

"Hello? Someone said something about a party?"

Molly rushed to greet her, wiping her hands again, unnecessarily on her apron and pulled her into a hug.

"Awww we missed you!"

"Missed you too, Molly. Oh my God, those sausage rolls smell amazing!"

As the women pulled out of their embrace, Laura spotted Dan leaning against the kitchen door frame wearing a half smile, with Buddy sat at his feet.

"Hey you," he said.

Leaving Chris to be welcomed by her godmother, she walked over to Dan, rubbing her hand on the dog's head.

"You okay? We good?"

"I'm good. We're good. You okay? We good?" His ever-present smile made her feel like she'd come home.

"I'm good. We're good," she said with a smile before they both burst into a fit of giggles and Dan pulled her into a hug.

"Missed you," he said quietly, so only she could hear.

"Missed you too."

"You gonna introduce me to your friend?"

Laura had almost forgotten Chris was there, making pleasantries with Molly. She took Dan's hand and led him down the short hallway.

"Chris, this is Dan, my best friend and adopted big brother. Dan, this is my boyfriend Chris."

Chris stood in the doorway, a masculine figure of a young man. His well-kept hair and neatly trimmed beard showed that he felt looks were important, but said little about the shallow character underneath, still trying to work out who he was. He was a few inches taller than Dan and broader by at least six inches but hidden behind the physique was a boy wanting to be a man. In contrast, Dan, casually dressed and very much at home in his own skin, radiated self-assurance and peace, at ease with himself and the world.

In a heartbeat, unnoticed by the younger man, Dan sized Chris up and decided he wasn't a fan.

"Nice to meet you, Chris. Welcome to our annual family party. Dan held his right hand out for the boyfriend to shake, still gently holding Laura's hand in his left.

"Nice to meet you too. Thanks for inviting me. Laura's told me a lot about you." The handshake he returned felt stiff, telling Dan that the younger man was wary of him.

"It's all lies mate, don't believe a word." Dan smiled at them both in an attempt to break the ice a little.

The potential awkwardness of the moment was averted before it could gather pace, as the rest of the two families descended on the hallway to greet Laura and her boyfriend. Dan allowed himself a moment to step back with Buddy and let them be the centre of attention, while keeping his eye on her. He always seemed to find her at the pinnacle of his vision for some unexplained reason. It was nice to have his friend back in the same house, albeit for a few hours.

*

As the evening went on, Chris was quizzed by everyone relentlessly, much to his amusement. Laura sat next to him the whole time so he didn't feel too overwhelmed. Dan couldn't help but notice the most contact they had was hand-holding. He imagined had he been Chris, he'd have been relaxing with Laura in his arms for most of the time.

Later, in the kitchen with Martin and Issy making drinks, Dan tried to avoid the topic even with Martin pushing him for more information.

"What do you reckon then?"

"She says she's happy, mate, that's all I care about."

"Yeah, he seems like a bit of a twat though, doesn't he?"

"Martin!" Issy slapped him hard on the arm. "Want to keep your voice down?"

"Ow!"

"You're lucky it's a smack on the arm and nowhere else!" She brandished her finger at him.

"Well I'm not wrong, am I?" Martin looked between Issy and her brother, waiting for them to acknowledge what they all knew was true.

"Let's give him a chance," Dan said, "as long as she's telling me she's happy, I'll support her."

"Jesus Dan, got splinters from that fence you're sitting on?" Issy rounded on him playfully.

"I can't win with you two!"

*

Chris Jones was trying his hardest to impress Laura's family and friends. She'd told him not to worry, that they'd like him anyway because they loved her, but he was still trying. He told them how he was studying economics, planning to progress onto working as an analyst and how he was the star of the university football first team. They all seemed to be impressed which helped to massage his confidence a little more; everyone, with the exception of the family dog, seemed really interested in him and it was a huge relief.

At various points during the evening, Chris spotted Dan and Laura talking together. She'd explained how close they were and how they'd grown up like siblings but it seemed a little off to him, how often they would hug and hold hands. She seemed to drift to him with ease and at least once he noticed Dan instinctively holding out his hand for her without seemingly knowing she was nearby. They had an odd synchronicity which left Chris unsure.

Dan had made an effort to speak to him about university and his hobbies which made Chris feel like he was genuinely interested, so it wasn't as if the older man was being standoffish. But when Laura was near her friend, she seemed to hang off him in a relaxed and easy way that she never seemed to do with him. It wasn't that he felt they were more than friends; it wasn't that. They were just familiar in a way Chris wasn't used to. It was weird and it made him wary.

*

The following morning as they lay awkwardly in her single bed at her parents' house, struggling for space and comfort, he had to ask.

"So you're close then, you and Dan?"

Laura's shoulders sank a little. She knew this was coming even though she'd already explained more than once how Dan was one of her dearest friends.

"Chris, we talked about this."

"I know. I'm just asking."

"He's like my big brother. I can't begin to explain how important Dan is to me and will always be. It's hard for me to even put it into words some days."

"Laura, it's okay. I'm fine with it."

"This isn't going to be a problem is it?"

"Of course not! I'm mature enough to be okay with my girl having a male friend. It's fine."

Laura felt as though that was just words without meaning but she wasn't about to dig deeper into an issue that she knew would ultimately only ever lead to one place. Leaning on his chest, trying to get comfortable, she wondered what Dan had thought.

She knew he would just want her to be happy but the deep desire to seek his approval left her doubting her decision to be with Chris.

They'd met in the spring term of their first year at uni. She knew he had a crush on her and while he wasn't really her type, Laura felt wanted around him and so she'd let things develop over the first few weeks after he'd asked her out. He was a bit awkward at times, trying too hard to impress her, but the attention was a welcome distraction from something she couldn't fully articulate.

Now, a few months later here they were, lying awkwardly on her single bed making stilted conversation. Part of her wanted Dan to message, as he often did in the mornings, but the panic of having to open a message from him right next to Chris filled her with a sense of dread.

"Right. Shall we get up and get some breakfast?" She said, tapping his hand in an expression of *get up, we're moving.*

Chris just pulled her tight a moment and slid his hand over her bottom. "Ah, come on baby, just five more minutes."

"Nope. Not happening. Not with my parents downstairs." She pulled herself from his clutches and climbed off the bed.

He reluctantly followed her, accepting that he wasn't getting any fun this morning.

Chapter 3

The Wedding

"Ready?"

"Ready as I'm ever going to be."

Martin France was clearly nervous, but standing with his best friend was helping to hold his nerves in check. All he had to do was wait for Issy to walk down the aisle and most of the nerves of the last twenty-four hours would be gone.

"Few minutes mate, then she'll be here." Dan was trying to reassure Martin, as was his job as best man, but he wasn't fully sure it was working. He was pretty nervous himself and it wasn't even his wedding day.

The doors at the back of the church opened and the organist flowed effortlessly from the filler music they'd been playing into *Here Comes the Bride*. Laura stood at the entrance with a smile on her face ready to lead the procession in. Dan smiled back. She looked beautiful as she glided down the aisle, wearing a stunning cornflower blue bridesmaid's dress, carrying a bouquet of wildflowers; her hair descending over her pale shoulders in perfect ringlets.

Martin visibly tensed next to Dan, who
gently placed a reassuring hand on his friend's shoulder.
"You got this mate," he said, never taking his eyes off Laura.
Once she'd taken her place opposite the men, they all looked back to see Issy on her father's arm, walking down the aisle flanked by their families and friends. By the time she reached her husband-to-be, Martin was crying openly at the magic of the moment.

*

As the ceremony progressed, Dan and Laura kept swapping smiles and side glances, with Dan attempting to make her laugh and giggle by pulling faces, winking and sticking out his tongue. Well-versed in their playful games, Laura only broke her straight face when, so distracted by trying to wind her up, Dan had missed the vicar asking for the rings. A glare from his older sister was enough to put him in check and back on his best behaviour.

*

"You'll get us into trouble one of these days," Laura said, as the bridal party stood together for photos an hour later.
"So I shouldn't do it?"
"I didn't say that Dan. All I said is that you will get us into trouble."
"I'll stop one day."

"You won't."

"I might."

Only when Chris joined them for the final full wedding party photo, did they curb their teasing of one another.

"You look sexy, baby." Chris Jones leaned in to kiss his girlfriend who turned her cheek to him, trying to nullify his overt public show of affection. As she did so, she noticed Dan looking away, focusing somewhere else.

"Thanks, Chris. Sorry I haven't seen you much yet. It's been busy."

"Ah it's okay. It'll be the same when it's our turn"

Next to them, listening in, the hairs on the back of Dan's neck stood on end and a cold shiver ran down his spine under his dress shirt. He felt a distinct desire to knock Chris on his ass and couldn't understand why. The sense that Laura stood to his right, was uncomfortable too, only made him want to do it more, as his vision darkened.

"Here you go, best man."

His attention was pulled away from the pressing thirst to tear Laura's boyfriend's throat out, by his dad, handing him a bottle of beer.

"Thanks, Dad." He watched her walking away with Chris, the photo opportunity finished, and his vision returned.

"He's okay. Try not to be too overprotective of her, Dan."

It's like his Dad could read his mind.

"I just want her to be happy. As long as she's happy, then I'm okay with it."

"She seems to be."

"Mhmm."

They sipped their beers in comfortable silence as they watched the rest of the wedding guests enjoying themselves.

"How are you feeling about your speech?" Dan asked.

"Ah, mine will be fine. I just need to speak from the heart and thank some people. But more beer will help I think." Brian laughed at the nerves they both shared ahead of their speeches. "What about you? You're the one who's under all the pressure."

"More beer, you say?" They both laughed. It was a good family day.

*

As his dad sat down to the applause of their gathered friends and family, Dan took a deep breath. There is only so much standing in front of the mirror that you can do to rehearse any kind of speech; he knew that he just needed to get on his feet and talk and hope to God he didn't mess it up.

Rising, he signalled for the attention of the rest of the guests by chinking his glass gently with his unused dessert fork, causing it to sing out across the room.

A hush gathered over the room and all eyes fell on him.

"I've been given strict instructions of what I am allowed to say and what I'm not, so out of respect to my best mate," he nodded to Martin further down the table, "and out of fear of my sister," he winked at Issy, "I shall behave myself."

The wedding guests around the room laughed fuelled by plenty of alcohol and his feeble attempt at a joke. Dan didn't care what caused it, he had their attention and was off to a good start.

"I have to say, Martin, to stand here on your wedding day is both an honour and a privilege and truth be told, one I didn't think I would have the opportunity to take. I genuinely assumed that my sister would have killed you by now." Another laugh from the room. He turned his attention to his sister.

"Issy. What can I say? All jokes aside, you look stunning and I couldn't ask for a better sister and friend." Turning to the room, he asked, "Can I ask everyone to raise their glasses to the gorgeous bride? To the bride!"

The room rose with glasses in hand and toasted Issy who smiled and blushed next to her new husband, whispering a thank you across the table to her brother.

"To the bride!"

Once everyone settled, Dan took another breath and looked around the room.

"May I also take just a moment to steal a little bit of Martin's thunder and toast the bridesmaid? I'm lucky enough to be one of Laura's best friends and while she isn't allowed to outshine Issy today," Dan rolled his eyes mockingly, to the delight of the rest of the guests, "she does look, I think you'll all have to agree, beautiful today and I apologise now for treading on her toes later during the dances."

He smiled as everyone raised their glasses again while he checked the notes of his speech which rested on the table in front of him. Laura blushed bright red into her wine glass and felt her heart racing and not only from being in the spotlight for a moment.

"I know usually it's customary for the best man to give a speech that's both funny and offensive to the groom but as those up here at the top table will agree, that's not really my style. So I wanted to speak from the heart instead." He cleared his throat.

"Love is a beautiful thing; I've been incredibly lucky to have grown up around it at home from the day I was born. Mum and Dad became our models for what real love is meant to look like. When people use the word love, it's usually associated with playfulness, kisses in the rain and summers that never end. Now while that is a part of it, there's always more to love.

Love is also fighting for what you believe in and being able to say the hard things at the right time to the person you share a life with. Love is being able to say sorry and mean it, forgetting all the things that went before it. Love is coffee being made for you in the morning, in your favourite mug, when you have to get up for work.

It's also looking after someone who's sick when the washing is piling up and you're missing deadlines because their being ill is your only priority. It's holding hands in the dark when you're both scared. It's not knowing the right words to say but knowing that your presence is what matters the most.

True love is forever and I know we live in a temporary world now, where love comes and goes." He subconsciously looked across the table towards Laura as he spoke. "But true love is for always because that person who completes your heart, is your home and you are theirs. Martin and Issy have found their home."

Dan turned to the room again and raised his champagne flute. "Will you please be upstanding once more and help me wish the bride and groom a happy forever? To the bride and groom!"

*

"You're pretty good at that, you know?"

"Pretty good at what?" Dan asked as he glided around the dance floor with Laura in his arms.

"Giving speeches and knowing the right things to say."

"Always the tone of surprise, Laura," he said, spinning her around, while the rest of their family and friends danced along to a slow Drake White song. "But thank you. I meant it, you know?"

"Meant what?"

"That you look beautiful today. If it wasn't Issy's big day, I'd say you stole the show."

Laura blushed and looked past Dan so as to not look into his eyes, which she knew would make her uncomfortable in a comfortable way. "You can say it anyway."

"And face the wrath of my sister on her wedding day?"

"Hmm, fair point," she said, chuckling.

"Have you had a nice day?"

"I have. It's been wonderful from start to finish and I'm glad we're getting to dance."

"I'm glad too. You always used to love me spinning you around the living room at your parents' house as a kid."

"It's one of many fond memories I have of us, Dan."

They danced in comfortable silence, just enjoying a few moments together as friends.

"I think if Chris has his way, you'll be next up the aisle."

"Chris can think all he wants. I'm not ready for any of that, and I doubt I will be for a while."

"When you're ready kid, not before."

"What if I'm never ready?"

"Then we will spend our lives dancing together at other peoples' weddings. Promise."

He could always break the tension when she could feel it building inside her, like taking away a spider from a scared child. He always made everything okay.

"You better not break that promise, Dan."

"I won't."

"You might."

"I always keep my promises, Laura."

In the corner of the room, Chris Jones glared at Dan dancing with his girlfriend. That should be his hand on the small of Laura's back. They should be his jokes she was smiling and laughing at. Those should be his eyes she was looking up into.

He knew they were just friends but a few drinks into the day wasn't helping him see that. All he could see was that Dan had a way with Laura that he, as her boyfriend, didn't have.

And it pissed him off.

Chapter 4

The Incident

As they entered the back bar of the Wheatsheaf, Laura squealed as she let go of Chris's hand and ran into Dan's arms. Although they hugged like any old friends would, Chris couldn't help but feel like this dude was holding onto his girlfriend a little bit too tight and for a little bit too long.

Pulling herself from Dan's embrace while still oddly holding his hand, Laura turned to her boyfriend. "Chris, say hello."

The two men shook hands, with Chris applying a little more pressure than was absolutely necessary.

Dan took the lead for her sake. "How's it going, mate?"

"Fine thanks, Dan. You well?" Cordial at best was all Chris felt like he could muster.

"Ah, it's a special day and I'm with my favourite people," Dan replied, giving Laura a wink as he spoke. "All is well."

*

Gathering with Laura's family to celebrate the news of their close family friend Issy being pregnant, was the third time that Chris had met Ben. The first time had been the previous New Year when she had taken him to the family home for their annual end-of-year party.

At first glance, they seemed as described, good friends who could easily have been confused for brother and sister but there was something in his girlfriend's mannerisms when she was with him that Chris couldn't get comfortable about and they touched each other *far too much* for his liking.

His feelings of angst over the two of them were only exacerbated the last time he'd seen them together at Issy and Martin's wedding, when he'd watched them dancing together. It was an itch that was getting worse and he couldn't scratch it. Every interaction they had only served to make him more possessive of Laura and he was beginning to feel like Dan needed to know who she belonged to.

*

As they had walked to the pub, that afternoon, Chris had raised his concerns but Laura had waved them away without a care.

"He's like my brother. Don't be silly."

But Chris didn't feel like he was being silly at all.

Sitting nursing his pint, Chris watched them talking like no one else in the world existed, play-fighting and hugging the whole time. He couldn't stand it. *And fuck if he heard Dan say...'you okay? We good?' one more time, he was going to lose his shit.* She'd barely spoken to him for the past thirty minutes; Laura was never as engrossed in the conversations they had, as she was with Dan. Subsequently, Chris felt abandoned at the end of the table while everyone else was having a whale of a time. *He's like my brother. Don't be silly.* Her echoing words didn't seem to soothe him but instead stabbed at him like a jagged shard the more he brooded into his beer.

*

An hour later, after lots of chatter and two rounds of drinks, Chris left Laura at the table with the family and the happy parents-to-be, saying he needed the loo but instead followed Dan, who had just stepped out onto the patio to take a call.

Dan turned as he hung up his call to see Chris standing behind him with a serious look on his face.

"You alright, Chris? What's up?"

"Look, Dan, I'm sure you mean well but you need to back off Laura."

"What? Is she okay?"

"She's fine! But just back off. I won't ask again."

"Chris, what the fuck are you talking about?"

"You and her!"

"Look I think you've got this wrong in your head."

"No, I don't. Just back off. She's with me and that's the way it is."

Chris made to leave, adrenaline still coursing through his veins like a spark along a trail of gunpowder, on a trajectory to ignite any moment. His fists balled without conscious thought as he started towards the door which led back into the bar.

"Mate, seriously we're just friends. I'm not a threat to whatever you think you have with Laura."

Chris turned. "I'm not your mate Dan, you'd best not think I am."

"Fine."

"Just back off her and stop all your being affectionate with her. I don't like it."

"Chris. We've been friends for as long as you've been alive. If she wants to hug me she can. You're just her boyfriend, you can't impose things like that, it's not fair to her."

"Look! Get this in your head! She's my girlfriend and I can tell her to stop it if I want to. Okay?"

"She's her own woman, Chris. You can't make her do something she doesn't want to do. If you love her then you'll accept that."

"Fuck off, Dan! Just fuck right off will you?" Chris's right hand pulsed in and out of a fist as he spoke.

"Seriously Chris, just walk away. All you'll do is end up hurting Laura if you carry on like this."

But Chris didn't walk away.

Making it seem like he was turning to leave for the second time, he dropped his right shoulder slightly and rather than moving away, lunged forward, his right fist connecting sharply with Dan's left cheek. He was no fighter and the blow was clumsily executed; had Dan wanted to, he could have easily swayed out of its path and beaten Chris to the ground. But as he watched the punch heading towards him, he knew that Chris needed this, so he just let the fist connect with his cheekbone.

Chris has expected his perceived adversary to go down and hit the deck, such was the macho bravado that he carried like a chip on his shoulder. To his surprise, Dan barely moved, instead just calmly wiped the blood away from the split of skin that had opened up a few centimetres beneath his left eye.

The next thing Chris knew, he was being pulled back by the shoulder, with Dave grabbing onto his collar.

"Back inside now!"

He considered swinging for Laura's dad too but his anger was fading fast and instead, he allowed himself to be manhandled back into the bar, Dave shoving him inside and closing the door as soon as he was through it. He then turned his attention to Dan.

"You okay?"

"I'm fine Dave, don't worry about me. He's just full of piss and vinegar. He'll grow out of it."

Dave took out a handkerchief and passed it to his godson.

"You could have retaliated and stopped his nonsense, you know that right?"

"Yeah, I could. But if I'd hit him, that would have only upset Laura more."

"I've half a mind to do it myself."

"He's not worth it, Dave. Just give me a minute to clean up and I'll come back in."

Dan's godfather nodded and left without another word.

*

"You did what?!"

Laura was steeped in fury, an emotion she rarely experienced or displayed.

"He baited me."

"Chris, I don't care if he stood out there with a bloody sign round his neck saying *hit me*, you had no right to do that!"

"I don't like how he is with you!"

"He's my oldest friend. How many times do I need to tell

you before you'll understand, he's like my brother!"

"Yeah, so you keep saying, Laura."

"Jesus Chris, how often do we need to have this conversation? Seriously this constant crap about me and Dan is getting tedious."

His bravado had all but deserted him at this point, so he just sheepishly looked away from his girlfriend's annoyed glare.

"Chris, you have a choice to make right now. Either come to terms with it and accept that Dan and I are friends or you can leave and not bother coming back!"

"I just love you, that's all."

"I know that but I can't keep going on like this."

Laura stood up, leaving him to mull over what she had said and walked away. She was done with Chris now and just needed to see Dan.

*

Stepping out onto the patio, she pulled her coat around her for warmth, even though there was little to be found. She was cold with simmering rage. He sat on the edge of one of the large sleepers scattered around edge of the patio area, dabbing a handkerchief against his cheek. Had the fight been the other way around, she knew Chris would have looked shaken, but Dan just looked like he was casually sitting down having a break.

Sensing another presence nearby, he lifted his eyes to see Laura standing in front of him.

"Sorry, kid."

"Don't you dare! Don't treat me like a kid right now!"

"Laura..."

"No, Dan! This is not how I wanted your sister's special day to go! What did you say to him?"

"Nothing. Honestly, he told me to back off from you and stop being how I am when I'm with you. He said he didn't like it and tried to hit me."

She sighed and sat next to him, lifting the handkerchief from his cheek.

"Looks like he made a decent attempt at hitting you." Her anger faded when she saw the blood oozing from the cut on Dan's face.

"I'm fine."

Gently folding the square of cotton to expose a clean section, she carefully held it to his injury.

"I'm sorry, Laura."

Dan didn't look physically hurt, just upset.

"He said you baited him." Her anger was gone for now and she spoke softly.

"If me telling him he can't stop you hugging me is baiting, then yeah, I guess I did."

"Thank you for standing up for me."

Dan pulled his mouth into the funny awkward shape he always did when he felt self-conscious.

"It's what I do."

"You'll look kind of rugged with a scar, you know?" The joke was meant to be harmless enough, she was just trying to make him smile.

But Dan took her hand gently, pulling it and the handkerchief along with it, away from his face.

"Laura, don't. Let's not give him any more ammunition than he already thinks he has."

"He can have all the ammunition he wants, Dan. I really don't care."

"He loves you, that's all. I can back off if you want me to. But that has to come from you, not him." The words feltlike acid in his mouth.

"There you go again," she said lovingly brushing her finger-tips lightly over the red mark that was growing around the cut, "saying stupid things."

"I'm serious. If my backing off means you don't have to deal with shit like that from him, then so be it. You know I only want you to be happy."

"You need to get this into that big stupid head of yours," she held her hand out at his eye level as she spoke. "It goes *you, boyfriends, everyone else*." Laura moved her hand down, as she punctuated each point.

He smiled but inside he also knew that this probably wouldn't be the last immature boyfriend he'd have to deal with in the future. The heaviness of that responsibility weighed on his heart.

"You gonna be okay?" She handed the handkerchief back to him.

"Yeah, I'll be fine."

"Right okay, I need to go back and deal with that one." She nodded to the patio windows where Chris could be seen, being spoken to by Dave. "Please don't stay out here too long. You'll get cold."

"I won't."

"You might."

"Okay."

"And I'll miss you."

Dan couldn't help but smile. "Okay, give me a second"

Laura headed back into the bar to face Chris.

*

Dave left the boyfriend looking shaken as she approached them, unzipping her coat.

"I'm not gonna ask what Dad's just said but you probably deserved it with your little display today." While the fury was gone, the annoyance at the whole sorry affair still lingered.

"I'm sorry, Laura. It won't happen again. I love you."

"I know that, Chris, but that's no way to demonstrate the fact."

"I know. Sorry."

Pushing the patio door closed, Dan realised he only had one available route to make his way back to his family and that was directly past Laura and her boyfriend. Accepting the inevitable and wanting to be the better man, he made his way in their direction, to the sanctuary of the table where he hoped his drink still remained.

"Dan, I'm sorry. I shouldn't have behaved like that." Chris held his hand out expectantly knowing it was what she would want.

"It's fine."

The pair shook hands and drew a line under the incident. Laura smiled but felt glad that she wasn't being forced into choosing between the two.

"Can I buy you a drink?"

For a moment, Dan felt like a whiskey sounded really good but as much as he wanted it, he knew adding further fuel to the fire of this potential powder keg was a bad idea.

"Thanks for the offer but I think we've probably all had

enough for a while." He wanted out of the situation as promptly as he could without seeming like a dick.

"I'll leave you both to it," he said, before picking up his glass and stepping away.

Ten minutes before, he would have affectionately placed his hand on Laura's shoulder as he went, even kissed her on the temple, that stuff was second nature. Instead, he now second-guessed things he'd done for a lifetime and quietly walked over to the larger table, where his family were sitting with Dave and Emily.

Chapter 5

The Other Woman

Laura stared in shock. This was wholly unfair and wrong and the look on Issy's face said fucking everything.

"Laura, let's just go in the front room, hey? It's okay. We'll get you a drink."

She knew Dan's sister was trying to get her away as quickly as possible, probably to try and explain but she couldn't move. Her blood boiled.

"Who. The fuck. Is that?!"

"Laura, come on. Let's get you a drink."

Issy hurried her into the living room of her parents' house and tried to explain.

"I didn't know until today. Apparently, it's a pretty recent thing. He met her through work."

"Why didn't you fucking tell me?"

Laura was raging. This wasn't right.

"I'm sorry, I know I should have said something, but to be fair I didn't think you'd react like this. You've been with Chris for what? A couple of years now? And he's only just met her. I thought you'd be okay."

"So who the fuck is she?"

"Her name is Chloe. He met her before Christmas in one of his training seminars. That's all I know. We're all as surprised as you are."

The visceral reaction she was experiencing was an assault on all her senses; she hadn't expected it at all, the shock taking her by complete surprise. Like a cornered and wounded animal, her eyes were wide and her nostrils flared. Laura wanted to scream and throw things.

"So what is this? He's going out with just anyone now?"

"Laura, breathe."

"I am fucking breathing," she snarled, through gritted teeth.

"You need to calm the fuck down. Chris will be here shortly and if he sees you acting like this, shit's going to go sideways."

Issy knew why Laura was raging so much but she had to try and dissolve this situation fast so the fallout wasn't catastrophic.

"She looks *nice.*"

"Laura, don't. She might be a really nice person."

"I'm sure she is, Issy." *Pft yeah right. She looks like a fucking tramp!*

*

Dan stood in the kitchen feeling guilty.

He'd seen how she'd looked at him, glaring over his sister's shoulder when she'd realised he wasn't alone. A part of him knew he should have told her in advance but he hated the idea of upsetting her, so like an idiot, he'd hoped that she'd be okay if they just turned up together.

But the look on Laura's face said it all. He'd fucked up big time.

"Babe, can you get me a drink? I'm a little thirsty."

Chloe Wilde was all limbs and sparkle. Her dyed brunette hair dropped low down her back, almost reaching her ass but it was mostly the result of cheap extensions. She'd spent more than an hour doing her make-up before they left Dan's house, perfecting the contouring on her face and applying ostentatiously large fake eyelashes. The gold outfit she'd worn for the party showed off her slim figure to the point where Brian had commented to his son that she looked like she needed a good meal inside her, not alcohol.

"Dad, for fuck sake."

"What? I'm just saying."

Brian Muir knew to just leave it alone and that they'd probably never see this Chloe again but had to just let it play out for the evening.

She was pleasant enough and said hello to everyone but simultaneously seemed to look down her nose at the Muir's home and the small kitchen where Dan and she were sipping drinks.

"Who was *that?*"

"That's Laura. I told you about her."

"Oh right yeah, the sister. She looks *pleasant.*"

"She's one of my best friends. I'll introduce you in a bit when she's finished saying hi to Issy."

"Can't wait to meet her. Maybe I could invite her to the gym.

Does she even work out?"

Dan's eyes burnt a hole through the living room wall to where Laura would be. *What the fuck am I doing?*

*

"I know I'm not his fucking girlfriend Issy, I'm not stupid. It's fine. He can date whomever he wants. I don't care. Just doesn't mean I'm exactly happy about a tramp being at our families' party."

"Laura, come on. Be nice."

"I'm perfectly nice. Look, I'll show you."

Laura stalked into the kitchen, the heavily pregnant Issy hastily rushing to follow her, abandoning her soft drink on the bookcase as she tried to catch up.

"Hi! You must be Chloe. So nice to meet you. I'm Laura."

Chloe raised her eyebrows and looked down at the 5'3" blonde standing a full eight inches shorter than her, who had appeared in front of her seemingly out of thin air.

"I'm Chloe, nice to meet you. Dan told me all about you. That you're like one of his best friends?"

"Yup. Well more like a baby sister really, so I'm in his life way more than just a best friend, you could say. So how did you two meet?" She was shaking as she spoke.

Dan stood sheepishly behind the pair as they passive-aggressively squared off. "We met at a training seminar a few weeks ago," he said.

He could see the venom in Laura's eyes as she looked from him to his new woman. "Oh, that's so cute. So this is new? That's sweet. I've known Dan my whole life."

37

"We know plenty about each other already, don't we babe?" Chloe giggled and winked at Dan who cringed inside, trying to avoid the daggers his sister was throwing at him from across the kitchen.

"Yeah. I'm sure." Laura smiled at Dan with as much falseness as she could muster. "Lovely to meet you anyway. Enjoy the party." Abruptly, she turned and left.

The look of triumph on the face of Dan's plus one said it all. Turning to him, she said, "Babe, I need to visit the little girl's room."

"Top of the stairs, Chloe - first door on your right."

Handing him her drink to hold in her absence, without so much as a please or thank you, she left Dan alone with his older sister.

"Issy. Don't say it."

"You're a stupid prick sometimes, do you know that?"

"How was I supposed to know she'd be upset by it?!"

"Because that sweet girl has been besotted with you her whole life and while she might be in some kind of relationship with someone else herself, that doesn't mean shit like this won't sting. You're such a fucking idiot, Dan."

"Wait! So she's allowed to date but I'm not? How does that fucking work?"

"Stop being dumb! You're allowed to date but be mature enough to not blindside her with it, for fuck sake. She deserves better than that. You know she's always had a crush on you, even if she isn't head over heels for you. You two are closer than any of us. You should have told her."

"I didn't think she'd be that upset."

"Well, she is. Fuck! I better go and check on her. Chris will

38

be here soon. This shit show of a New Year's party doesn't need to get fucking worse."

Buddy who'd been lying quietly in the corner of the kitchen, decided this was the moment to leave, following Issy back out of the kitchen and staying near her for the rest of the night.

*

As the evening dragged on, Dan kept Laura and Chloe apart as much as he could without arousing suspicions. Laura kept herself close to Chris the whole night, something her boyfriend was happily surprised with. She seemed unusually overly affectionate and he was basking in her attention, although he had to admit, Dan's new girlfriend was fit.

Chloe, for her part, became progressively more bored as the lacklustre party wore on.

"Babe, come on, let's go to the club and have some real fun. I feel like I'm at a kid's party."

"We'll go soon. I promise. Just need to stay a little longer."

"Fine. Whatever." She sighed and rolled her eyes and even when Dan looked at her in annoyance, she didn't tone down her attitude. She just wanted to go somewhere more entertaining and if she had to upset a few people to get her own way, so be it.

*

Around 10 pm, Laura was in the kitchen topping up her drink and having a break from Chris; being with him was exhausting sometimes and tonight was one of those occasions. But she was bringing it on herself. Trying to put a brave face on the situation meant she had been dripping herself all over him and she felt slimy as a result.

She put the top back on the bottle of Coke and turned to find Dan walking through the kitchen door. They looked at each other and her blood began to boil again.

"Don't worry, I'm going back to the other room."

"You don't have to. Stay, I was just coming to get some more drinks."

"It's fine. I don't want to be around you much anyway tonight."

"Laura."

"What, Dan? Don't you have *that* to get back to?" She waved her glass in the vicinity of the living room.

"Her name is Chloe. Come on kid, don't be like that."

"Oh don't you fucking dare call me that."

"Laura, come on. Please."

"You could have told me. I called you yesterday and you didn't have the balls to tell me. I never thought you were a coward, Dan."

"How was I meant to know you'd be upset by it?"

"You should have known! You should have cared enough about me to know!"

"I do care. More than anyone!"

"Well, this is a funny way of fucking showing it!"

"Laura, I'm just seeing her, it's not serious like you and Chris. It won't affect us, I promise."

"Whatever, Dan."

Laura started to move towards the door but Dan stayed fast in her way. He needed to fix this.

"Laura, please. Let's not fall out over this."

"Oh, I'm fine Dan. You want to date some skinny girl? Go ahead. Be my guest. Just don't expect me to be happy about it."

"She's nice enough when you get to know her."

"Right. So that's your type now?" Laura's lip quivered as she felt uncomfortable in her own skin for the first time in years.

"What's that supposed to mean?"

"Stick thin. All fake hair and ridiculous eyelashes."

"She's a nice person."

"Right."

"Laura, please. I don't behave like this with Chris."

"And what do you mean by that!?"

"Nothing."

"No no, come on Dan. Use your words like a grown up!"

"It's just, you know, I've never really been his biggest fan, maybe less so after he hit me!"

"Well, it doesn't matter what you think, does it? 'Cos *I'm* his girlfriend."

Laura's fury was reaching boiling point. She wanted to scream and hit him. It felt like he was someone she didn't know any more.

Dan tried to hide the hurt of her last comment. A part of his heart took the wound in a way he didn't expect and he struggled to keep his cool.

"I'm not going to fight with you about this Laura. It's my life. I can see whoever I want."

"Yeah just don't expect to see too much of me, if that's how you're going to spend your time."

"Laura!"

Just then Chloe walked back in to find them standing off in the kitchen. Laura didn't bother to look at her, instead keeping her eyes on Dan with a look that was a mixture of fury for his actions and pleading with him to take the pain away.

"Babe? Where's my drink?" She didn't even glance at Laura, instead just stood in front of Dan in an attempt to get his attention. "Come on, let's get out of here and have some real fun. I'm sure your *little* sister will understand."

"Okay Chloe, go wait outside. I just need to say goodbye and get Buddy, then we can leave."

The taller girl giggled and although he never took his eyes off Laura, she kissed Dan on the cheek, and went to get her coat, not even bothering to say goodbye to the rest of the family as she left, shutting the front door behind her.

Laura stared at Dan and felt her whole world crashing down around her. There was too much inside that she was trying to fight against. Tears, rage, and love all swirled around in her as she felt hate for the man she'd loved her whole life. The betrayal was more than she could bear.

"Laura."

Reaching for the locket around her neck, the one he'd given her for getting into uni, she tugged it from her body, snapping the chain.

"Save your breath, Dan!" She said as she shoved it into his chest and held it there, digging it into his skin. "Keep it. I don't want it anymore."

He reluctantly took it from her as she left, storming upstairs. He'd broken her heart and he knew it. Nothing in the world could ever feel worse to him or ever would. This was the moment in Dan's life, he would reflect decades later in old age, that was his biggest regret.

For a moment, unsure of his next move, he wanted to turn back the clock. Hating himself, he sighed and pocketed the small silver locket before apologising to his family and Laura's parents, grabbing a confused Buddy and leaving with Chloe.

Chapter 6

The Locket

"Y ou sure it's a good idea you being here?"

Emily Gray looked at her godson and sighed. Her daughter had locked herself away in her bedroom since her boyfriend Chris had left first thing in the morning to go back to his parents for lunch. They only knew the full facts of what had actually occurred the night before, when Issy had called to check up on her friend earlier that day.

"I need to see her, Emily. I have to try and put things right."

"Okay, come in." She stood aside as he came in and he stepped into the living room to find his godfather watching TV.

Dave looked over his reading glasses at him. "You're either brave or stupid Dan. I wouldn't want to face her in the mood she's in but I'm glad you're here. You two aren't meant to be like this."

"I think I'm a bit of both, truth be told, Dave. I just hope I can fix this."

Climbing the stairs to her room, Dan felt sick. He disliked confrontation at the best of times but knowing he'd hurt Laura so badly, made the idea of this particular encounter even worse.

Her bedroom door was shut, so he tapped gently with his knuckles. A few seconds later the door opened slightly and she looked up at him.

"I don't want to see you."

"Please. Just give me a few minutes. We need to talk."

"Fine," she said, walking away and letting him open the door the rest of the way himself. This was going to be hard but Dan knew he deserved it.

Laura sat on the edge of her bed, wearing a baggy jumper and matching joggers. She'd pulled her hair back into a ponytail only because she'd gotten sick of it getting in her face as she cried. She looked and felt like a mess and just wanted to hide.

"Say what you have to say and then get out. I want to be left alone."

Dan stood at the door, leaving it open, to give her space. "I'm sorry."

"Fine. You done? Good. Now you can leave." She wanted him gone. It was too hard seeing him there.

"I ended things with Chloe last night after we left. I don't want to have anyone in my life that causes you to react like that. I'm sorry I didn't tell you in advance that I was bringing someone."

Her lower lip eased itself out and she began to well up; the pent up emotions still raw and on the surface.

"Laura, I'm so sorry. The last thing I ever wanted to do was to cause you so much hurt. I should have treated you better and shown you the respect you deserved."

She wiped her eyes with the sleeve of her jumper and sniffed away a sob. "It fucking hurt. Seeing you there with her. I know I have no right to feel like that but it's the truth. She's everything I'm not and even though you and I are only best friends, she made me feel insignificant to you and I hated you for that."

"You will always be more important to me than anyone else, Laura! I was an idiot. I'm so sorry I've made you hate me."

"I don't hate you. I hated you. There's a fine line between love and hate and last night you pushed me on the wrong side of it."

"I know. And I'm sorry."

"But you didn't have to end it with her. I would've gotten over it."

"Anyone who provokes a reaction like that in you has no place in my life."

Dan moved to the bed and when Laura didn't show any reluctance, he gently sat himself next to her.

"How can I fix this?"

"Dunno."

"No one is more important to me than you Laura. You know that, even when I fuck things up."

"That's not how it felt last night. I felt like I was nothing in your life, which I know is stupid because I should be able to let you be with whoever you want to be with." She cried openly as she spoke, her hands drawn back into the sleeves of her jumper. "But seeing you with her was a shock I was not prepared for and it made me feel jealous. Not because she had you but because I was scared she'd replace me."

"I can promise you right here and now that *nobody* will ever replace you in my heart, *ever.*"

She leaned herself against his shoulder and cried some more.

"It scares me how much you mean to me."

Dan wrapped his arm around her and pulled her into his chest, cradling her head in his hand. She fell into him and sobbed into his chest, resting her hand on his warm comforting body as the tears fell.

"You'll always be my first priority, Laura. Always. I will protect you and keep you safe from anything, even if that thing is me. It goes *you, girlfriends, everyone else.*" He moved his hand down as he punctuated each point, echoing the gestures she'd made at Issy and Martin's gathering.

"I know I shouldn't be this upset. It's not as though you're Chris, but I don't know, that's the first time I've seen you with anyone else for a while and it just really got to me."

*

Dan hadn't dated for a long time. It wasn't something that even interested him really. He had a great job, a lovely family and brilliant friends, and he had Laura so he didn't really feel like he'd needed to date as well.

He'd known Chloe wasn't the one but it had been fun to have someone new to hang out with for a few weeks, even though she wasn't really his type.

Now he felt like he could happily never date again and that would be fine, he just wanted to see Laura with her beautiful smile back on her face.

*

"You okay? We good?" He asked.

"No, I'm not okay. But we're good. I'll be fine. Promise."

He kissed the top of her head as she snuggled into his chest and he wanted to stay there forever or at least until she was okay again. The shame of how he'd treated her sat on his chest like a monstrous weight, and nothing seemed to be able to take him out from under it.

All of a sudden, as she seemed to be calming down, Laura wailed.

"My locket! Dan, I broke my locket."

The memory of tearing off the locket he'd given her and making him take it back, didn't feel anywhere near as satisfying now as the action had the night before.

"Hey, it's okay, don't worry."

"No! It's not! I never take my locket off! God Dan, I'm so sorry I broke it." She was inconsolable.

"Laura, stop. It's not broken."

She pulled herself upright and looked at him, tears streaming down her face. "What? But I snapped the chain? It's broken."

"You did snap it but I've already put it on a new one for you. It's not broken anymore."

With that Dan reached into his jacket pocket and pulled out her little silver locket, letting it dangle in his fingers. As it spun in the light, it sparkled just as it had the first time he'd given it to her. Instinctively her hand went out to touch it.

"Dan! How?"

"Issy had a spare chain that was essentially the same as the one that got broken. So we swapped it out this morning. When I gave it to you before you went to uni, I told you that it was yours forever, no matter what and I meant that."

He handed it to her and she lovingly rubbed her thumb over it as it rested in her palm. Of all the gifts she'd ever received in her life, this was the most special. She'd never even taken it off until last night. It was as much of a part of her as Dan was and she adored it.

Her tears ran down her face as the heaviness of the previous hours began to lift.

"Want me to?" He gestured towards her neck and she handed the little silver locket back to him and turned, scooping her ponytail out of the way so he could return it to its rightful place. Once it was back around her neck she held it gently and smiled.

"Thank you," she said quietly as she leaned back against him.

"I'm sorry, I drove you to take it off."

"It's okay. It's done now. You're both back where you belong and that's all I really care about.

"Me too." He wrapped his arms back around her.

"I'm sorry you two split up."

He smiled. "No, you're not. And neither am I."

She knew it was true.

"I don't need a girlfriend. I've got you."

"Well, I'm not putting out Dan, I'm telling you that now."

She was feeling more like herself and the playfulness was returning.

"I should hope not! A fine upstanding lady like yourself, shouldn't even know what that means."

"I'm as pure as the driven snow, Dan."

"Sure you are." They laughed and the sound filtered through to the floor below them.

*

Dave looked at his wife and they smiled at each other.

"Seems like the universe is back on track," Emily said, relieved that things were okay again.

"And it seems like I'm still in the game!"

"Dave, you two and that silly bet!"

He winked at his wife and grinned. "Don't tell me you're not secretly hoping I win!"

She rolled her eyes at him but knew he was right.

"Tea?" She asked.

"I'll give you my last Rolo."

*

"Do you have anywhere to be today?" Laura asked, as she relaxed back into Dan's embrace.

"No, not really. I'd like to stay if you want me to?"

"Yeah. I'd like that. Fancy taking Buddy for a walk?"

"Go for it. I think the fresh air will do us both good."

"Ok right, well let me sort my face out and we'll go.

A few minutes later, they were heading out of the front door together with Buddy on the lead and Laura's parents smiling behind them, watching them go.

Chapter 7

The Drink

As they walked, the events of the previous evening dissipated and both of them visibly relaxed.

The afternoon was cold; the crisp winter air prickling at their skin which caused Laura to hold onto Dan's arm and pull herself into his body for warmth. She felt like the pieces of her that had been broken the night before were back together and she couldn't help but smile.

"Did Issy shout at you?" Laura asked.

"Last night at the party. Last night when I got home. And then again this morning. Yeah, she's made her feelings abundantly clear."

"Sorry."

"Don't be. I deserved it. Even Dad told me in no uncertain terms that I was in the wrong."

"Wow, you must have really gotten it wrong for your dad to pull you up."

"Mhmm," he smiled, relieved to have Laura back close to him again. The words his dad had spoken about how he should treat the people he loved better, screamed in his head like a wailing siren.

"Don't worry. I still love you." She said, pulling herself ever closer to him.

"I know. I love you too."

They spent a comfortable hour just wandering along in one another's company and letting Buddy sniff every lamp post he came to. As they neared the house upon their return, Dan didn't feel ready to let her go just yet.

"When's Chris back?"

"Erm, tomorrow night I think. Why?"

"Fancy coming over for dinner tonight? We can hang out and watch some TV or something? Maybe we could just get a takeaway? My treat."

Laura smiled. "I'd like that, yeah. Let me just go in and tell Mum and Dad, then I'll grab my bag and we can go."

"Okay. Cool." Dan's usual half smile was threatening to explode all over his face as he stared at his feet.

She left him to put Buddy in the car as she tried to quell the happiness that was ready to burst out of her.

Opening the front door and rushing up the stairs, she called out to her parents.

"Going to Dan's for dinner. Be back later!" She grabbed her handbag from her room and rushed back down the stairs to find her mum waiting by the front door.

"When will you be back?"

"Later. Not sure when, think we're getting takeaway."

If it was any other man, Emily Gray would have stopped her daughter in her tracks and issued some sort of warning about being careful, but she trusted her godson implicitly.

Before she could say another word, Laura was out of the door calling back, "love you mum. See you later."

Emily just smiled and watched her go, waving to Dan who was smiling from the driver's seat of his hatchback.

*

With Buddy curled up on the armchair in Dan's living room, settling down for a post walk, afternoon nap, Laura and Dan hung up their coats and walked down the long hallway to the kitchen.

"Want a drink?"

"Oh yes please, I'm frozen!"

"How about I make you a hot chocolate?"

Laura chuckled. "Dan you're back in my good books, you don't have to keep laying it on thick."

He shut the cupboard door where he was just about to take the hot chocolate powder from, and smiled at her.

"No no, I still want one," she grinned.

Five minutes later, she sat in front of a sight of complete deliciousness. Dan had made her a thick hot chocolate with steamed milk using the steam wand on his big coffee machine, topping it all off with squirty cream and little marshmallows. The heat from the combination of the drink and the mug was causing the cream to run down the sides, and she was having trouble keeping up with catching every bit of lost cream as it leaked slowly down the sides.

"Want more cream?" He asked, before moving to put the can back in the fridge door.

"God, unless you're planning to squirt it directly into my

mouth, I'm not sure where you'd put it? This cup is already full to overflowing!"

He brandished the can at her. "Open wide then."

"You think you're funny and that I wouldn't let you, but you'd be wrong."

Dan walked over to her with a quizzical yet expectant look on his face. She looked at him as he moved closer and opened her mouth, her eyes displaying the smile her mouth was unable to show.

Without pomp or ceremony, he shot a generous amount of cream into her waiting mouth and watched it run down her chin.

She had to push him away to get him to stop as they both laughed, with Laura choking on copious amounts of squirty cream, so much so her eyes were watering.

"You're such a dick!" She spluttered.

"Yeah but you love me so it's okay."

As the afternoon turned to evening, they sat watching reruns of their favourite sitcom and sharing an extra-large pizza he'd ordered for them. With her feet up, resting on him, Laura had nearly fallen asleep, full of food and with a happy heart but it was only when Dan had gently shaken her leg to stop her drifting off into dreams, they both realised it was time to take her home.

"Call me tomorrow?" He asked, walking her up to her parents' front door a little while later.

"Always. God, I feel like I'm going to sleep well tonight."

"Makes two of us."

"Thank you for today, Dan. For all of it. Not just for your

time and the pizza but also for rescuing us when I thought we were lost"

He dragged her into a big hug and she threw her arms around him.

"I'm always going to be here, kid and I'm always going to fight for us, especially when it's hard. My life wouldn't be the same without you. And you forgot about the hot chocolate!"

The door clicked open behind them and she turned to see her dad standing there, smiling.

"You two okay?"

Laura looked at him and smiled but kept herself snuggled into her friend's chest.

"Yeah. We fixed it."

"I'm glad."

The men shared a look between them, in appreciation that everything was back to normal. Dave winked at his godson and nodded as Laura relinquished her hold on Dan and slid into the house.

As he drove away, he felt a huge sense of relief that in the last twenty-four hours he hadn't lost the singular most important person in his life.

Chapter 8

The Arrival

Maximus Benjamin France, Max for short, was born the following spring to very happy Issy and Martin. While the labour had been long, the exhaustion and pain soon faded as Dan's sister held her newborn son in her arms for the first time, with her emotional husband standing next to her. Weighing in at a solid 8lbs 5ozs, Max was very much an ethereal baby boy with bright hazel eyes and a cheery disposition.

Two days later, with Issy back in the comfort of her own home and with Martin frantically running around trying to make sure everything was taken care of, it was decided that mother and baby were feeling up to receiving visitors. Her parents and brother Dan were knocking on the door as soon as they had been given the green light to enter.

Molly Muir cooed over her grandson while Brian held Max's little fingers in his and tried not to cry like a blubbering idiot.

"You can hold him, you know?" Issy said, looking at Dan who was patiently waiting his turn.

"I know. But let Mum and Dad have their moment." He

smiled, it was a good day. "Anyway here, I got him a little something. I hope it's okay."

Dan passed Issy a gift, wrapped in soft pastel blue paper.

"Oh you really didn't have to."

"Yeah, I did. He's my nephew. And you're my favourite sister."

"I'm your only sister, Dan."

"Yeah, that too but you're still my favourite," he grinned.

Issy unwrapped the present and held it up in front of her.

"Dan! I love it! It must have cost a fortune!"

In her hands, she held a mini NFL shirt belonging to her brother's favourite team, with the number 1 emblazoned on the front, and the name Max in big white lettering on the back.

"Only the best for my little dude. I think it's a bit big for him yet but it'll fit soon enough I'm sure."

A knock at the front door an hour later, drew a tired Martin from the sofa and signalled the arrival of Dave, Emily and Laura Gray who were as excited as Issy's family at the new arrival. Hugs and presents were exchanged and they joined the Muirs to gather around the proud yet exhausted parents.

"Where's the baby?" Laura asked, looking around the front room of family and friends. "You two are great and all, but I am only here for a baby cuddle!"

Issy smiled and nodded to the conservatory. "He's with his uncle in there. I think someone's a bit smitten."

Without a word, Laura positively skipped off to find her friend and baby Max.

As she got close to the conservatory, she could see Dan through the partially open sliding doors. He was holding his nephew in one arm and with the other, he was holding Max's fingers while bouncing him gently with his body. She could hear him talking softly to the baby, saying he'd always be there for him, whenever he was needed and that they'd be going to see his favourite NFL team together as soon as his nephew was old enough.

Something in Laura stirred as she watched him and realised that Dan with a baby was as natural a thing as summer after spring. She felt like he would one day make a wonderful father and a part of her ached happily at the thought of it, even though she wasn't sure where this feeling was coming from. Her own body hummed with a yearning that was as old as time.

She gently slid the door fully open causing him to turn and smile at her. He spoke in hushed whispers, not wanting to wake the sleeping baby.

"Hey you."

"Hey. Who's this little guy?"

"This is my nephew, Max, but he's going to be Maxxy to me." The pride and love on his face was as evident as any emotion he'd ever shown. Laura melted next to him as she stroked Max's hand with her fingers and pressed herself closer to Dan.

"Congratulations Dan. Hey, little Maxxy." She smiled, resting her head on his shoulder as they cooed over the baby boy in front of them. For the first time in her life, the idea of maybe one day having her own babies didn't frighten her and standing in warm comfort next to Dan, she couldn't help but wonder.

"Oh, it's all Issy. I'm just a very proud uncle right now."

"Uncle Dan. It suits you."

"What does that make you then?"

The pair smiled and relaxed into the joy of holding a newborn as if they were proud parents themselves. It was only when Issy knocked gently on the patio door did they realise they still existed in the real world with other people.

"That would make you Aunty Laura," she said as she walked in.

"Issy, he's beautiful."

"Thanks, Laura. I'm not sure my body agrees right now but my heart very much does."

"Was it bad?"

"He came out bum first so I feel he's destined to be a pain in my life forever but he's perfect so it's not all bad." Issy looked tired even though she was grinning. "It is, however Uncle Dan, time for this little man to have something to eat."

Reluctantly but very carefully, Dan handed his precious nephew back, while keeping hold of his tiny fingers for a moment longer.

"So there's actually something I wanted to talk to you both about and now is as good a time as any."

Dan and Laura looked at each other curiously and then back to Issy standing in front of them.

"You both mean the world to Martin and I, and we know you're going to be a big part of Max's life, so we were hoping that you'd agree to be his godparents."

Laura squealed only to be shushed by Dan and his sister. "Oh my god! Yes please!"

"It would be an honour Issy, thank you."

"Good! Right, I'm taking this boy upstairs to feed him, I'm trying to get the both of us into some sort of routine."

"Ah Issy it's fine, stay, don't be embarrassed, we're all grown-ups."

"I'm not embarrassed little brother. Trust me. You'll have seen much worse, I'm sure. It's just that he's brand new and I'm new to this and we are still getting used to one another and sorting out latching on. Give us a day or two and he'll be eating at the table with the rest of the family - we are just taking ourselves upstairs while our meals still come with a side order of frustration and tears."

She left to feed Max in the comfort of her own space as Dan and Laura remained awhile in the conservatory.

"So godparents. That means you're stuck with me now, you know that don't you?"

"What, like forever? Forever is a long time, Dan."

"Are you complaining, kid?"

"I think you're misunderstanding my question for a complaint."

"So you're okay with being stuck with me for a lifetime?"

"I'm not answering that," she said, taking his hand. "Come on, let's go see everyone."

Smiling Dan let her lead him back to the rest of his family and hers, savouring the warmth of her touch for a few precious moments. Today was a good family day.

Chapter 9

The Ride Home

"Erm Laura, what car does this Dan of yours drive?"

Laura's flat-mate, Rachel stood at the front bedroom window looking expectantly down over the road below.

"He's got a black hatchback. I'm not sure of the make. I think it's a Ford. Why?"

"Because a really good-looking middle-aged guy just pulled up but he's not in a hatchback."

Laura sighed, put her wash bag on the bed where she was packing up the last of her things, ready to leave her uni home of the last three years and got to her feet.

"Rach, if you're going to do this every time an older guy shows up, I'm never going to finish packing and anyway, it won't be him; he's not middle-aged you fuckwit, he's 31!"

She moved next to her friend and peered out through the window. At first, she couldn't make sense of what she was seeing. There stood Dan, in his usual black T-shirt and stone-

61

washed blue jeans and next to him sat Buddy, but he'd just jumped down from a huge black pickup truck that dwarfed the other cars on the street.

The single cab truck sat on huge tyres and the roof was adorned with so many lights that it took her a few seconds to count them all. She watched as Dan reached into the passenger seat to retrieve Buddy's lead, and clipping it to his collar made to walk up to the front door of her university accommodation. She wasn't able to see his eyes as he kept his RayBans on, shielding his sight from the bright morning sunshine but just seeing him outside made her happier than she'd been in a long time.

She smiled, excitedly. "It's him! That's Dan."

Rushing out of the door to meet him, she was greeted by an excited Buddy, desperately trying to escape the short leash Dan held him on.

"Buddy! Chill! Sit down!"

"Ah he's fine, he's just missed me that's all," she said, dropping to her knees to fuss the exuberant Border Collie, who proceeded to lick at her face as she scratched him playfully behind the ears.

"Yeah and you've probably missed me too but you're not jumping all over me, licking my face! Buddy. Sit!"

His co-owned dog finally listened to the instruction and promptly sat on his bottom, panting hard with excited energy.

"Well if you wait your turn Dan, maybe I will!" She smiled at him as she got back to her feet.

"Sure you will, kid!" The grin on his face said it all. He'd missed her and he was as happy as the damned dog now sat at his feet. "Come here will you, don't make me wait for my hug."

"So needy, Dan!" She flung her arms around him and for a second exhaled, in the same way someone would arriving home after a long time away. Everything felt right with the world.

As he pulled his arms from her to end the embrace, which was now being watched by the flat-mates he was yet to meet, Laura turned into him and slowly licked his face from jawbone temple, ensuring that she got as much of his face wet as possible.

"You're such a fucking child!" He said, laughing.

"Yeah but you love me so it's okay."

Wiping his drenched face with the back of his hand, Dan looked at her. "Right, shall we get your stuff loaded so we can get this road trip started?"

"Erm yeah but first, you can explain," she pointed over his shoulder, "that!"

He turned with a grin. "Well you didn't think I was getting all your shit in my car, did you? And I wasn't about to drive up here in some boring white van, was I? No my dear, if we're doing this, we're travelling in some semblance of style!"

Laura felt anxious as she looked on.

"Don't worry. I'll help you up." He slid his free hand into hers and squeezed gently, taking away her nerves in an instant.

"Right, let's get you introduced to Rach and Georgia, then we can get my stuff packed up and hit the road."

"Lead the way."

The three of them turned and headed inside.

"So you're the famous Dan?"

"I'm not sure if *famous* is all that applicable but yeah I'm Dan, pleased to meet you."

He politely shook hands with Georgia, Laura's other flat-mate who smiled and appraised the man in front of her.

"We were concerned she was making you up to start with but when she wouldn't stop talking about you, we figured you must be real. I feel like I know you, Dan, such is the amount I know about you!"

"Georgia, know when to keep your mouth shut!" Laura glared at her soon-to-be ex-flat-mate and at this particular moment in time, very questionable friend.

Dan blushed and grabbed a box marked *Laura* from the kitchen counter behind Georgia, and took it out to the truck.

As he walked away, she watched him go.

"Seriously Laura, you had that at home and you opted for Chris? If I had a piece of meat like that back home, I'd have never come to uni in the first place!"

"I didn't have anything, meaty or otherwise, Georgia. He's like my big brother."

"Right, so you won't mind me asking him for his number then?"

A rush of fiery jealousy flashed in Laura. "You have a boyfriend!"

"Ah, sweetie it's always good to have a reserve or two"

Laura wanted to scowl at her friend but she didn't, instead, collected another box of kitchen objects that would be coming home with her and left Georgia to her thoughts, whatever they were.

Out by the truck half an hour later, Dan was letting Buddy drink from a bottle of water before starting the ride home as he waited for Laura. She was saying a long goodbye to Rachel and Georgia by the entrance to what had been their home for three years.

After a few minutes, she wandered over to him with tears welling in her eyes. Taking her last bag, he carefully placed it in the bed of the black pickup truck and took her hand.

"You okay? We good?"

"Yeah, just a bit emotional. It's the end of an era, isn't it? We're good."

"It is. But it's also the start of new beginnings for you."

"I know." She took a deep breath and smiled at Dan. "Shall we?"

"Let's."

He opened the passenger door and let Buddy jump up into the cab and settle himself in the footwell. When the dog was clear of the door, he flicked a small step down on the side of the cab and turned to Laura while still holding her hand.

"My lady," he said, gesturing her into the truck.

"Smooth, Dan. Real smooth."

"Would you rather I just grab you by the ass and shove you in?"

Laura smiled at him. "Not in front of the girls." Stepping onto the small platform she climbed up into the pickup. It had that new car smell and she couldn't help but feel spoilt.

As Dan pulled out of the parking space and headed out slowly across the university campus, he flicked on the inbuilt entertainment system on the dashboard.

"Right, shotgun rules apply. We have just over two hours till we get back to yours, you're in charge of the music; it's Bluetooth so just connect your phone and there's a bag of sweets and snacks behind your seat."

"You have this all planned out?"

"Everything with intent, Laura." He winked at her.

"You're too good to me, you know that right?"

"How else am I meant to treat my favourite person in the world?"

Laura smiled and took out her phone, connecting it to the Bluetooth before opening her music app. It didn't take her long to find the playlist she wanted to listen to for the journey.

"You have a playlist called Dan?" He was surprised to see his name flash up at the top of the list of songs on the screen in the centre of the dashboard console.

"Mhmm. It's all songs that I like and ones that have memories of our times together. It's got some good tunes. Is that ok?"

"I mean, would it be okay if I had a similar playlist on my phone called Laura?"

"You do?"

"I might." He grinned and she knew he did; the idea of it made her heart flutter.

She hit play and they sank into familiar songs for a while as Dan drove them off campus and out towards the motorway, Buddy resting his head in her lap; her fingers gently stroking his head. A part of her wanted them to drive like this forever and never go home, so it could be them together like this with Buddy for always. but she knew that real life wasn't like that.

Laura kept stealing glances at him as he drove. He looked relaxed with one hand on the top of the steering wheel, his right arm resting lightly on the open window of the driver's door. Dan looked at home in the truck even though he'd never driven it before today. As with everything he did, he seemed to be totally at ease with what he was doing as he casually scanned the lanes of the motorway in front of him through his black RayBans.

Just being next to her friend brought Laura a stillness she could never really find elsewhere in her life. She felt as though this was not only a safe space but like curling up wrapped in a warm blanket, sitting in your favourite chair. It was just a feeling that was right. There weren't any other words for it.

They shared a bag of jelly sweets as they drove, enjoying the sunshine and the music as the world eased by outside.

A new song came on and Laura went to skip it immediately.

"Whoa! No no no! No skipping songs."

"Yeah well, this one is an exception."

"What, because you think it's embarrassing?"

She blushed next to him and scrunched her nose up. Looking away, she replied quietly, "It is embarrassing."

Dan smiled. "This is one of my favourite songs, kid and one of my favourite memories of you. So while you might feel embarrassed by it, I personally love it and how it makes me feel."

*

Iris by the Goo Goo Dolls held particular memories for both of them. At Dan's 21st birthday party, he'd opted for karaoke with his friends and family as a bit of fun. Most of the singing had been awful, mostly due to the alcohol that fuelled the confidence of those holding the microphone.

Little Laura, at only eleven years old, had wanted a turn and Dan, being her biggest supporter, had thought it was a brilliant idea. Picking one of his favourite songs, she'd nervously waited her turn.

"Hey. You'll be great. Feel the fear and do it anyway, remember?" He'd said as he squeezed her hand.

Laura had sung her heart out in front of a room full of people.

Even though she'd been out of tune and out of time for the duration, Dan had cheered her on the whole way through even coming to sing the last chorus with her. He'd been the perfect big brother.

It was only years later when everyone had told her how bad her rendition was, that the shame of experience had crept in. However, on some level, this hadn't stopped it from being one of her favourite songs, even if she had vowed to never sing it again.

*

"*And I don't want the world to see me. 'Cos I don't think that they'd understand.*" Dan sang at the top of his lungs as he turned up the song using the controls on the steering wheel.

Laura looked over at him.

As the song went into the guitar solo, Dan looked back over.

"Either sing with me, or I'll put it on repeat for the rest of the entire journey!"

"You're incorrigible!" She smiled.

When the final part of the song kicked in, Dan started singing loudly again.

Fuck it! She thought.

"*And I don't want the world to see me*

'Cause I don't think that they'd understand
When everything's made to be broken
I just want you to know who I am"

For the first time in years, they sang in unison. It wasn't award-winning but it was Dan and Laura being explicitly themselves, together and it was perfect.

*

An hour later, Dan pulled the truck up in front of Laura's new house, where her boyfriend Chris waited.

"Traffic okay?" He asked as he started reaching for the boot of the pickup, Dan approaching him from the driver's side.

"Yeah fine."

Chris dragged out the biggest box he could get his hands on from the back and made a show of carrying it inside the house.

Dan made his way around to the passenger side to let Laura out. He opened the door and she swung her legs up over Buddy's head and dangled them out of the vehicle, smiling.

"My lady," he said, holding his arms out to her.

She leant out a little and placed her hands on his shoulders as he held her gently at her waist. In an easy movement, he supported her as she hopped down from the seat she'd spent the last few hours relaxing in. As she came to rest on the ground she bumped into Dan slightly.

"You okay? We good?" He asked quietly.

"Mhmm We're good." Laura could feel her cheeks flushing.

"Welcome to your new home."

She sighed but there wasn't complete contentment in it.

"You two gonna just stand there? Or are we going to get this stuff unloaded so Dan can take this truck back?"

Chris stood behind them at the front door.

Laura fell back into reality. "Yeah. Sorry. Let's get everything inside."

It didn't take them long to unload her things, placing everything in the living room, and soon Dan was ready to leave.

Kissing Buddy on the head, Laura told him she'd see him tomorrow to which he let out a loud and enthusiastic *Woof!*

"I'll come over in the morning and pick him up."

"Sure, I'll be in all day."

"Sorry, Dan. Just feel like it will be a bit hectic here tonight, that's all."

"He'll be absolutely fine at mine this evening and don't be sorry. I've always said he's our dog so at times like these it's okay for him to be with me. Don't worry. Just get yourself moved in and settled and you can come pick him up whenever you're ready."

They hugged briefly, much more fleeting than their first hug of the day at the university, before Laura awkwardly pulled herself back.

Sensing that this was how it would probably be now between them, Dan stepped back and smiled as best he could.

"Message me later?" He asked.

"Yeah. Promise."

"Good."

"Dan?"

"Yeah?"

"You okay? We good?" She could feel unwanted emotions starting to bubble on the surface.

Dan could tell she was struggling with the idea of this being her life now.

"I'm okay. And we're good, always. I'll be right here kid, okay? Anytime you need me, I'm just a phone call or message away. That will never change"

"Thank you."

Dan stepped away and around to the driver's side door, climbing in. Starting the big V8 engine, it roared into life. After checking his mirrors, he turned to look at Laura through the passenger window and winked before pulling away and off down the street.

Laura's eyes stung as she watched his tail lights getting further away down the street before he disappeared out onto the main road.

Her heart sank as she turned back inside to continue unpacking.

Chapter 10

The WTF

Dan paced his living room feeling restless. The clock on his home hub read 3:17 am and he'd been awake for at least an hour. As someone who naturally had a very active brain, late-night bouts of insomnia weren't uncommon for him but tonight while awake, he was thinking about the night to come.

It was technically New Year's Eve, although only by a few hours, and an evening of celebrating with his family and the Grays lay ahead of him. And that of course meant seeing Laura.

As the years had passed since that night she'd kissed him foolishly in her parents' kitchen, a deep-seated niggle had developed that he'd found himself unable to quite shake. He'd started looking at her differently, jealous of what Chris had in his life, and finding himself wanting to be around Laura more and more. Now, knowing he was about to spend an alcohol-fuelled evening with her, only seemed to make his brain go into overdrive.

Pausing to rest for a moment, he slumped on the sofa and

closed his eyes, hoping it would slow his mind down.

*

The party had started as many had done before it, hugs and catching up, accompanied by drinks before everyone seemed to naturally drift off into smaller groups for the evening. With the grandparents fussing around little Max, Martin and Issy were relaxing in one of the big armchairs, leaving Dan and Laura to gravitate to their usual spot in the kitchen; enjoying a few drinks and some good company.

"Almost time for you to pin me against the kitchen counter and try to kiss me like usual, Laura…" Dan flicked his eyebrows at her from the other side of the kitchen.

She couldn't help but chuckle at the dig. "In your dreams, stud. You had your chance," she said, shrugging nonchalantly. They both laughed.

She looked perfect leaning against the doorframe in her snug-fitting black dress, the only pop of colour coming from the silver locket around her neck. Her permanent reminder of the two of them. Together.

He stood opposite her in a black fitted T-shirt and dark jeans, his gaze seemingly heating up the room.

"You look good, Laura," he said casually, sipping his drink as he spoke, his eyes raking down her body, appreciating the woman in front of him. Her blue eyes sparkled and hid the rising nerves behind the steely gaze she held on him. Her blonde hair fell softly onto her shoulders, let down from its usual ponytail in a way that Dan loved. He let his eyes drift, following the lines of her dress and stood in awe at every curve and fold accentuated in the tight-fitting garment.

She coyly toyed with a strand of hair and bit her lip. "I could say the same about you."

His T-shirt hung on his body like it was tailor-made, the muscles in his forearms and the size of his hands drawing her attention.

"Do I get a kiss at midnight?" He asked, walking towards her.

"Do you want a kiss at midnight?"

"Why do you think I'm asking?"

His eyes seemed to lock onto her soft pink lips as she nervously looked up at him. He took her drink from her hand and placed it on the counter beside them and replaced it in her grasp with his own hand, pulling her to him.

Letting out a little squeal, she gently bumped into him, never taking her eyes off him.

"We should wait till midnight..." she gasped as his hands melted into her back.

"We might."

"And yet...."

Dan tugged her closer to him and placed his lips against hers. His hands slid up her back and then into her hair. His body pressed against hers as the heat surged in both of them. From the second their lips met, it was heated and passionate, with each of them longing for exactly what was happening. Dan was claiming what he wanted and Laura was giving it freely, knowing that this was everything she needed.

He spun her sideways and pushed her up against the kitchen counter as they kissed; hands all over one another's bodies.

They didn't care that they weren't alone in the house, all that mattered was each other and the urgency they both felt.

Dan's fingers found the zip at the back of her dress and tugged gently as her tongue slid over his. Rather than fully undoing her dress, he just loosened it enough to allow him to pull it from her shoulders, giving him access to her pale skin which he touched with his lips and teeth in a way that made Laura's legs go weak. Throwing her head back she stifled a moan as Dan seemed to be finding all her buttons and repeatedly pressing on them until they broke.

As he worked his lips over her neck, dragging whimpers from her throat, Dan's hands teased up her thighs, pushing her beautiful black dress with them and quickly it was bunched around her hips. Letting go of the material, he quickly slid his hands up her sides and continued up under her arms, not stopping until he was lifting her up onto the countertop, where she landed with a bump. She grabbed him and pulled him close, kissing him hard, wrapping her legs around his waist, literally pleading with him not to stop what he was about to do.

*

What the actual fuck!

Laura woke with a start and sat up in bed, panting. Her body was on fire, as her mind raced. Every part of her dream had felt real and the urge to rush to Dan and recreate it was stronger than any desire she'd ever had.

As she caught her breath, Chris snored unattractively next to her. Not wanting to disturb him and face awkward questions about why she was awake, sweating and gasping for air, she quickly shuffled out of bed, making her way quickly to the bathroom. She needed space to cool off physically and mentally.

Splashing water on her face, Laura looked at her reflection in the mirror and quickly lost herself to visions from her dream. This hadn't been the first passionate dream she'd had of a man who looked like Dan, but this definitely was the hottest and the one where it definitely was him without ambiguity. Her body ached as she stood looking at her mirrored reflection.

Jesus. That was hot!.

Deciding that getting back into bed with Chris felt wrong on so many levels, she took herself down to the sofa and grabbing a blanket, decided to sleep there. Or at least try. She checked the time on her smartwatch. 3:28 am. The annual New Year's Eve party was still hours away but she didn't know how she'd even be able to look Dan in the eyes for at least six weeks after this.

The longing she felt was both familiar and confusing as she lay down and tried to relax. She wanted to text him but didn't want to wake him up. They'd always had this quirky thing where they'd so often be awake at the same time, like some weird cosmic synchronicity that kept them in step with one another. She picked up her phone.

Laura: Looking forward to seeing you at the party tonight x

A reply came straight back, making her smile nervously.

Dan: Can't sleep either?

Laura: No. Woke up from a dream and now I'm awake but I should try and doze at least. x

Dan: I'll let you try and get back to sleep. My brain is buzzing and I feel like I need to go have a shower or something to calm down. Miss you.

Laura groaned quietly at the thought of him in the shower and then remonstrated herself from the guilty pleasure.

Laura: Miss you too. Msg me later when you wake back up if you manage some more sleep. x

She put her phone down and rolled over on the sofa. As she closed her eyes, she pushed away the clearly inappropriate thoughts and wondered if her black dress would still fit.

Chapter 11

The 'After' Party

Laura woke up on the sofa and groaned. Everything seemed to hurt with an unsatisfied ache.

"You okay baby? Why did you sleep down here?"

Chris handed her a cup of tea which she really didn't fancy.

"Erm, I was awake in the night and didn't want to disturb you so came downstairs for a bit. I must have fallen asleep without realising. Sorry."

"Don't be, it's fine."

"What time is it?"

"Just gone ten."

"Fuck. I need to walk Buddy and get over to Mum and Dad's. I'm meant to be helping Mum sort the food out."

"There's no rush. I can walk Buddy if you want?"

He's being nice, why is he being nice?

"No it's okay. Chris. Thanks though. I'll sort him. What time are you heading off?"

Her boyfriend had plans to spend New Year's Eve with his own family as he hadn't had the chance to see them so far over the Christmas break.

"Just after lunch if that's okay?"

"Mhmm. Of course." She was partly relieved he wouldn't be around tonight. Flashes of her dream about Dan were still striking brightly in her mind like forked lightning.

"Well, I'll go jump in the shower first if that's okay then? Unless you want to join me?" He leered at his girlfriend who tried to hide her discomfort at the idea.

"I'm still half asleep. You go shower. I'll wake up with this cup of tea and then go walk Buddy. I can shower later."

"Okay baby. Whatever you like."

With that Chris left her to her cup of tea and unbeknownst to him, a mind full of Dan. She sunk into the sofa cushions and wanted to go back to sleep but a wet nose found her cheek and it brought her out of her thoughts, making her smile.

"Just you and me at the party tonight, boy. You better be a good date and treat me nicely." Her fingers scratched behind his ears.

Her phone buzzed on the floor at her feet. Picking it up she saw it was from Dan.

Dan: Morning. You okay? We good? You get some sleep?

Laura: I'm okay. Just waking up actually. We're good. You okay? We good? How was your shower? X

She shouldn't have asked that and cursed herself after hitting send.

Dan: I'm okay. Been up a little while. Just wanted to check in and make sure you were okay. We're good. Never made the shower. But ended up falling asleep on the sofa.

Laura: Makes two of us. X

Dan: What time are you getting to your Mum and Dad's today?

Laura: In a bit. Need to walk the dog and then get dressed for tonight. So probably after lunch. How about you? X

Dan: Around five I think. Going for lunch at Issy's first and then I'll head over.

Laura: Looking forward to seeing you. X

Her body was still simmering from her dream hours before; it was taking all her self-control not to bite her lip and take a moment for herself.

Dan: Me too. See you in a bit x

Turning to the Border Collie at her feet who was now assaulting a chew toy, Laura decided she had to get up, lest her urges take hold.

"Right. Come on Buddy. Let's get you walked before I make us late!"

*

Stepping out of the shower after lunch, the house to herself now Chris had left, she was annoyed that she'd been so distracted with her thoughts that she'd washed her hair twice and forgotten to condition it. Her head was full of moments from last night's dream and what that meant for the evening ahead.

She had no idea how she would even look Dan in the face after what she'd experienced the night before. Worryingly he'd always had the ability to know what was on her mind over the years and it terrified her that he might figure out where her head had been, hours before. Coupled with that fear, her body was aching with a desire that just wouldn't leave her alone for a second.

After she'd dried her hair and straightened it for the evening, she'd pulled her black dress off the hanger and slipped it on, checking her reflection in the full-length mirror on her side of the bed.

As she studied her body in the glass, she couldn't shake the curiosity of how Dan's hands would feel on her.

*

After a few distraction-filled hours at her parents' house, Laura was relaxing in the kitchen, having spent the afternoon helping her mother sort out tray upon tray of food and sweet treats. She was particularly proud of the way she'd arranged the plastic wine glasses into a pyramid on the dining table.

She checked her watch. 5 pm.

Right on cue the latch on the front door clicked.

"Hey. Did someone order a tall, handsome man? I have a delivery here."

"No, not today thank you," she grinned at Dan as he

unzipped his coat.

"Come here you."

She practically skipped over to him, Buddy following in her footsteps as he arrived from the front room; her nerves and memories of steamy dreams were gone for a moment as she hugged him.

"You okay? We good?" He asked. It was their thing. And no one else dared to use it.

"I'm good. We're good. You okay? How was lunch? We good?"

He placed a kiss on her forehead, relieved at not having to restrain his affections as Chris wasn't present. The kiss sent a shiver all the way deep into her core. "I'm good. Stuffed full of roast beef. We're good."

She patted her hand into his chest and stepped back. "Good. Right."

Dan sensed the uncomfortable shift in her but let it go.

Later in the evening, the traditional annual Gray/Muir party was in full swing. The night was going as many had done before it, hugs and catching up, accompanied by drinks, before everyone seemed to naturally drift off into smaller groups for the evening.

With both sets of parents fussing around little Max, Martin and Issy were relaxing in one of the big armchairs together, full of roast beef and buffet. This left Dan and Laura to gravitate to their usual spot in the kitchen, enjoying a few drinks and some good company.

"You okay kid? You seem a bit distracted tonight. We good?"

Laura knew he'd end up figuring out something was amiss.

She felt seen and she really didn't care for it.

"I'm fine. We're okay."

"Wait, what? We're never just okay. What's wrong?"

"Nothing. Honestly, we're good."

She poured herself another drink and Dan left it alone.

She started up a conversation about Buddy and how he needed his checkup with the vet in a few weeks and for a short while, they talked about that. But Dan wasn't having any of it.

"Look, if something's up, just tell me okay?"

"Nothing's up. Just leave it, okay."

"Laura, what is it? I can tell something is on your mind."

"Please, Dan. We're good. Promise."

She could feel the tension building rapidly in her.

"We said we'd always tell each other the truth. What's so bad that you don't want to tell me about it? Is it Chris? What did he do?"

"No! It's nothing to do with Chris."

The anxiety was starting to overwhelm her and she wasn't sure she could keep it under control much longer if he kept this up.

"Then what? I'm worried about you."

"I had a sex dream about you! About us! There! Happy?" It rushed out of her mouth before she had a chance to stop it and she quickly clamped her hand on her mouth to stop any more stupidity from escaping.

Dan was taken aback but smiled.

"Was I any good?" He asked, smiling and walking over to her.

"Fuck off!" She laughed, hitting him hard on the arm with a

huge grin on her face. The tension from the day evaporated in an instant.

"Qw! Look, it's fine. That stuff's normal. Healthy even."

"Okay maybe, but Jesus, it's not something I want to experience with him lying next to me."

"Well no, but still, was I?"

"You're such a dick you know that, right?" She couldn't help but laugh at him as he raised his eyebrows at her. "Fine. Yes, you were. But I'm saying nothing more about it."

He hugged her and she relaxed into him, appreciating that he hadn't been panicked by her confession.

"And anyway," he said softly in her ear, "I've had similar dreams about you, don't worry."

Pushing him away, shocked but pleasantly surprised, she looked up at him. "Dan!"

"What? I said it was normal!"

"Was I any good?" She asked, biting her lip.

"Oh and I'm the dick?!" Dan feigned indignation and smiled a little half-smile.

"Well? Was I?"

"I had more than one dream, didn't I? What do you think?" He winked at her and lovingly pulled at her hand to draw her closer.

"Oh no you don't! No more hugs for you, I know where your mind has been."

"Hey, yours has been in the exact same place!" He remonstrated, pulling her into a hug as she simultaneously turned her back into him.

They stayed there for a moment, each of them wondering if this position was really a good idea or not. Both of their minds went to places of longing for a second before Dan brought them back down to earth with a bump.

"Love you," he said, licking her face.

"Fuck sake, you're such a child!" She said, laughing at him.

"Yeah but you love me so it's okay."

"What are you two up to?"

Issy had walked in to top up her drink, only to find Dan hugging Laura from behind and licking her face.

"Nothing," he said, quickly letting go.

"Yeah, we were just messing around," Laura added, straightening her hair and dress.

"Sure you were." His sister smiled at them both. "It's okay, you two, just be you. I'm not here to judge. I think it's sweet really."

Laura cleared her throat as she turned away, hoping flushes of blood in her cheeks would pass quickly. Dan leant back on the counter with his hands in his pockets.

"Erm, I'm just gonna pop to the loo." Laura smiled, as she rushed out of the increasingly claustrophobic kitchen.

Issy looked her brother in the eye.

"Issy. Don't say it."

"Hey," she raised her hands in surrender, "I'm saying nothing."

He scrunched his face up awkwardly.

"Ah, you look a bit flustered Dan. Something *up?*"

He smiled at his sister and shook his head.

"Fuck off, will you."

Issy just laughed and picked up another can of mixer and the half-drunk bottle of Archers and went back to Martin, leaving Dan to his embarrassment.

Chapter 12

The Question

Max squealed so hard, it felt like every glass and window in the house might shatter.

"Dan! Jesus! Will you go easy with him, you'll tire him out for later!"

"Uh oh Maxxy, Mummy's being boring again."

"Dan!"

"Love ya sis!" Dan raced out of the kitchen holding his excitably squealing nephew upside-down by the ankles.

"I'll kill him. I will actually kill him dead." Issy fumed at her mother who was buttering bread for sandwiches.

"He's just like your dad. I had to regularly stop him from throwing you across the room onto the sofa when you were Max's age. You used to love that game though."

"Didn't Dad throw me into a wall once?"

"Yeah, the game stopped after that!" Molly laughed at her daughter who looked panic stricken.

"Martin! Don't let Dan throw Max around!"

Max's fourth birthday was, as usual, a family affair. Once

Issy and Martin had done presents and breakfast with their much-loved son, her brother and parents had turned up by mid-morning to join in the fun; her dad staggering in weighed down with presents, which the already excited Max went crazy for.

When all the gifts had been opened and shredded paper lay strewn across the living room carpet, much to Issy's dismay, he turned to Dan.

"Uncle Dan, where's your present?"

"What present, Maxxy?"

"My birthday present, silly!"

"What? It's your birthday?"

"Yes! I'm four!"

"Oh. I didn't realise mate."

"Uncle Dan! I know it's behind your back!"

"What is? Oh this?" Dan pulled out a hand wrapped gift from behind his back. "This is my pillow."

His nephew squealed in excitement.

"Max, calm down," his mother told him gently.

"Happy Birthday, Maxxy." Dan bopped the soft present on the boy's head and handed it over.

The four year old did what all boys that age do on their birthdays, and made short work of the unwrapping.

"Mummy! A new shirt! Look, Mummy look!"

Max waved a new NFL shirt at his mother who smiled back at her brother.

"He'll love it Dan, thank you."

"Mummy Mummy! I want to put it on like Uncle Dan." Max pointed to his uncle who was wearing his own matching dark blue jersey.

Later that morning, in their matching team shirts, Dan and Max were causing a ruckus around the house and loving every minute of it, while preparations were being made for lunch.

The front door opened and a soft voice sung out through the house. "Where's the birthday boy?"

"Aunty Laura's here!" Max leapt out Dan's lap and rushed to the door.

"There's my favourite little man!" Laura said, gathering her godson up into a huge hug, covering his face in kisses which caused the boy to giggle.

"What did you get? Come on, show me your presents! Wow, is that a new NFL shirt? Now, who would have given you that, Maxxy?" She teased him as he beamed with pride.

"Uncle Dan did. It's just like his!"

"Of course he did." A mumbling Chris stood behind his girlfriend in the doorway.

"Come on Max. Show us what you got for your birthday!"

She put the birthday boy down and was promptly dragged by the hand into the living room with great urgency by an impatient Max. As she took her coat off, she saw Dan smiling in the armchair.

"Hey you." He didn't get up to greet her. In recent years their usual affection was muted whenever they were around Chris. It just wasn't worth the drama, but it still made them both sad.

"Hey you. Playing the best godparent game again I see?" She smiled at him.

"Ball's in your court, Gray."

As she focused on Max, who was showing her present after present, she sat herself on the couch across the room and tried to listen intently to her bouncy godson, but could feel Dan looking at her and Chris.

"Maxxy, do you want my present?"

"Our present, baby," Chris reminded her.

Max dropped the toy in his hand without a single care and made his way over to his godmother.

She held out a large box which she handed over to him. It was so big, Max almost couldn't be seen behind it. Chris sat on the arm of the sofa next to his girlfriend, grinning smugly.

Excitedly, the birthday boy placed it on the floor and kneeling in front of it, promptly tore into the wrapping paper, pulling open the box. Digging his little hands inside, he lifted out a bright white football.

"Thanks," Max said, immediately putting it back in the box. He turned around and picked up a new box of Lego from his pile of presents.

"Uncle Dan, can we make this please?"

"Of course Maxxy. Let's go do it at the table, yeah?"

The boys headed to the table and started to build, leaving Laura looking anything but surprised, sitting with a now visibly pissed off Chris.

"What kind of boys don't like football?" He muttered.

"Ones that grow up watching American Football with their dads and uncles. I told you to get the NFL ball."

Her boyfriend just huffed to himself and looked sullen, an expression that didn't really leave him for the rest of the day.

After lunch, Dan was in the kitchen alone, putting used paper plates in the bin when he felt a pair of soft familiar hands wrapping themselves around him.

"Hey you," she said.

He smiled and turned pulling her into his chest. He breathed in the familiar scent of vanilla.

"You okay? We good?" He spoke softly into her ear.

"I'm okay. We're good. You okay? We good?"

"Always when you're here, kid."

Laura melted into him for a moment before pulling herself away before they got into trouble.

"Looks like Chris wasn't impressed."

"What did he expect?" She replied, rolling her eyes. "I told him not to get that fucking football but he didn't listen."

"You gonna be okay?"

"Yeah don't worry. Aunty Laura got her favourite little man a little something just from her. I'm all good."

Dan chuckled. "Why am I not surprised?"

She smiled at him. It was so good to see him. Even though they spoke all the time and tried to make as much time as they could for each other, moments like this when it was just the two of them weren't as frequent as they used to be, so she savoured them.

At that moment, Max came running in and extended his arms to Laura wanting his Aunty to pick him up. As she did, she mockingly groaned, "oh Maxxy you're getting so big I'll not be able to pick you up soon!"

That made the boy laugh and he nuzzled into her neck.

"You okay little man?" His uncle asked, as he brushed his hair tenderly out of his face.

"Mhmm everyone else in the snug." He rested his little head on Laura's shoulder and smiled.

"Uncle Dan?"

"Yeah?"

"If you're my Uncle and Aunty Laura is my Aunty, why aren't

91

you married like Mummy and Daddy?"

Both Dan and Laura stared at him and then each other, shocked and open mouthed.

"Erm…because…well…" Dan stumbled over his words as Laura suppressed a surge of giggles and looked away. "You see…what it is…"

"Maxxy." Laura stepped in to rescue the situation before Dan drowned and went down with the ship. "Me and Uncle Dan are your Aunty and Uncle because we're your godparents."

"Mummy said you were like my spare parents but why aren't you married? Don't you love each other? Daddy loves Mummy a lot!"

"We do love each other." She paused looking at Dan. "Just not quite in the same way."

"But the important thing is Maxxy, both me and Aunty Laura love you very much and always will." Dan leant in and kissed his nephew's forehead.

The three of them stood there in the moment, full of love in the kitchen. The only person, other than themselves, who knew they were even there was Chris, who could see them through the door from where he sat in the snug. His heart hurt a little at something he knew deep down would never be his. It further darkened his mood for the rest of the day.

By late afternoon, Max was fading fast with birthday tiredness and everyone started to make their way home so that Issy and Martin could get the boy calm and ready for bed.

He'd waved goodbye to nearly everyone except his uncle who was staying to spend time with Martin when the front door opened.

"Hey, Maxxy." Laura stood in the hallway, having told Chris she'd forgotten something, making him wait impatiently in the car. Issy walked through to her, carrying her son in her arms.

"You okay, Laura?"

"Yeah just got a little something for Max. Just from me." She winked at him and smiled.

He took the present that she handed to him and began to awkwardly open it.

As Max looked down, his eyes widened and he smiled a big toothy smile.

"Mummy look! It's me and Uncle Dan!"

Issy looked at the framed picture in his hands. A very proud Dan, holding Max in his arms, both wearing matching NFL shirts. She welled up uncontrollably.

"Laura, it's beautiful."

"You like it Max?" Laura asked.

"Yes! Thank you Aunty Laura! Mummy, can I put it by my bed? Please?"

The women smiled at each other as the boy beamed at the gift in his hands.

When Laura had said a final goodbye and gone back to the car, Issy carried her son into the kitchen.

"Everything okay?" Dan asked, standing by the sink.

"Yeah, Laura just dropped off a present for Max that's all."

"Another one?" He playfully rolled his eyes as his nephew held out the picture frame to his uncle.

Taking it from his chubby little hands, Dan looked down, his heart swelling with emotions.

He took in the photo of himself, holding his nephew, both of them smiling brightly; a part of his soul wishing that the image also included the woman who'd given Max the present.

Chapter 13

The Game

"**M**um! Dad says I can only stay up till half-time. That's not fair!"

Max France was disgruntled. He'd been working on his parents for days in an attempt to convince them to let him stay up for the big game, even though it was a school night. Uncle Dan was coming over and he wanted to stay up with him and his dad; to be one of the boys and watch the Super Bowl. Something they did every year together. He was pinning his hopes on this being the first year he'd be allowed; he was seven now and surely that was old enough?!

"He did?" Issy questioned her son. "That's funny because I told Dad that you couldn't see any of the game. So it looks like you have a choice to make doesn't it?"

"Please Mum! I promise I'll go straight to bed after the game. Please!"

"Max, the chances of you making the end of the first quarter are slim." Martin had overheard his son's pleading with his mother and had decided a united front was the way to go.

"I'll do all my homework next week."

"You'll do that anyway!" His mother laughed like it was the most ridiculous thing seven-year-old Max had ever said.

The front door opened and Dan stepped in. Before he had a chance to even say hello, his nephew was on him.

"Uncle Dan! You'll let me stay up for the game won't you?"

"Sure Maxxy."

"NO!" Martin and Issy shouted in unison.

Dan looked caught in the headlights.

"Erm. Best ask your parents, mate. Sorry, I feel like I'm outnumbered here."

Max, realising he wasn't getting anywhere, stormed off up the stairs to his room, in a show of defiance that the very bright boy hoped would make the adults left downstairs feel guilty; hopefully guilty enough to let him stay up way past his bedtime.

"All okay in the France household?" Dan asked.

"All good, baby brother, just the curse of having an emotionally intelligent son who's desperate to hang out with his uncle."

"So he's not staying up for the game?" He was a little sad at the possibility of Max missing out.

"He's staying up till half-time, mate."

"I didn't agree to that!" Issy was perfectly okay with her son staying up just this once, but she wasn't about to let Martin think he'd won this particular battle.

"Ah, come on Issy. He's worked really hard at school so far this term. He's earned this." Her husband's pleas extended from his mouth to his eyes.

"Yeah, come on Issy. He can sit with me and chances are he'll be asleep before the end of the first quarter." Dan was on full reserve for his best mate.

"Fine."

"I love you, babe." Martin stepped closer and kissed her on the nose.

Dan hung his coat on the back of a kitchen chair and pulled off his bobble hat. "I wouldn't go that far, but you're alright though," he said, winking.

"Well, he's your responsibility all night. I don't want you whining to me if he starts being a problem for you both. Laura's coming over for a girls' night."

"Laura's coming?" Dan said that a bit too quickly.

Issy smiled at her brother. "Yes. Is that a problem?"

"No. No problem at all." He could feel his body temperature rising rapidly as beads of sweat started to form on his chest. *Maybe I have too many layers on.* "Erm, I just didn't think she was coming. When I spoke to her earlier, she said she was going out tonight but didn't mention she was coming here."

"Maybe you should ask more specific questions, Dan?" She replied, full of mirth.

"You okay, mate? You seem a bit flushed?" Martin knew between him and his wife they were prodding a bear, but it was fun and they weren't about to stop.

"I guess we should order enough pizza for Chris as well then." Even though he knew the chances of Laura's boyfriend wanting to actually come and watch sport played without a round ball was slim to none, Dan hoped that they'd confirm his absence.

Martin groaned. Issy raised her eyebrows.

"Babe, he's a little twat and we'll have to spend the whole game explaining the rules to him! Again!"

She looked between the men and shook her head ruefully.

"He's not coming. You're both safe for the night."

"YES!" Martin and Dan said in unison, while simultaneously high-fiving each other.

As the boys made their way to the snug to set up camp for the evening, Issy called her brother back into the kitchen.

"Did you see it yet?"

"See what?"

"Laura's new tattoo?"

"No, not yet. She told me the appointment was yesterday, but I haven't seen it. Why do you ask?"

"Oh, no reason."

"Issy, don't be a dick. Spit it out."

"Just wait and see Dan."

He sighed, exasperated and shook his head.

"Oh don't worry, it's not anywhere or anything risqué. It's a nice tattoo." She moved to walk past him and placed her hand on his shoulder as she did. "I think you'll like it."

By 8 pm, Laura had arrived and was sitting with Issy, sharing a bottle of wine and swapping gossip at the kitchen table, with Buddy sitting at her feet as she'd not wanted to leave him at home; the boys playing games in the snug waiting for the Super Bowl game to start.

Without Chris in tow, she'd been more relaxed with Dan since arriving and they'd been hugging and teasing each other from the word go. It was just who they were at their core.

"Mum, can I have a drink please? Dad says I have to ask you." Max's broad smile reached his big hazel eyes.

Issy pulled a face at Martin's distinct lack of ability to make any kind of parenting decision alone.

"A small one. And it's your last before bedtime mister, so don't guzzle it."

"Thanks Mum!" Max said, making his way to the fridge to get a juice carton.

Laura smiled as she watched her godson. He was growing up so quickly and was a joy to be around; she loved being with this family so much, and it just made her long for her own in the future.

Max turned to her and giggled.

"'S'up Max?" She asked, with a look of mock confusion.

"That's not your hat."

"What hat?"

"Aunty Laura, that's Uncle Dan's hat and you know it is."

"Oh, this?" She said pointing to the NFL themed bobble hat perched on her head. "No, this is my hat." She winked at him.

Max whipped around the table in a flash, scooped it off her head and legged it out of the room to return the hat to its rightful owner, laughing loudly the whole way.

Laura chuckled as she watched him run away.

"He loves you, you know?"

She turned and looked with apprehension at Issy.

"Max, I mean." But she knew who her younger friend had thought she'd meant.

Laura quickly regained her composure. "He's a lovely little boy and I love him just as much in return."

"Mhmm," Issy smiled to herself as she sipped her wine.

*

"So, can I see it?"

Dan and Laura sat together in the snug while Max and his

parents were upstairs sorting bath time and getting him ready for bed, before the game started.

"Do you want to see it?

"I might."

"You don't?"

"You know I do."

She smiled and passed him her drink to hold. "Please?"

He took the glass and watched as she pulled her hoodie off over her head, and proceeded to ball it into her lap. She then turned her back towards him, spinning on the sofa cushion, before sliding a hand under her t-shirt, pulling it to the side to expose the skin of her left shoulder.

As Dan looked, he found it hard to breathe. Etched into her skin in gorgeous black cursive ink, were the words from his favourite song. *Take a hold of your dream.* The needle had left slight ridges where it had worked through her delicate skin just above her shoulder blade and he reached out, gently brushing his fingers over it without thinking.

"My song."

'It's something that means a lot to me, Dan." She turned back to look at him, breaking the soft touch of his hand on her skin.

"Sorry. Is it sore?"

"No, not really," she smiled. "You like it?"

"Laura, it's beautiful."

She started to pull the hoodie back on and wished she was instead sliding herself into his arms for the rest of time. As her head emerged from the neck of the garment, the idea of that cleared and she was back in reality which was considerably less appealing. A shyness came over her as she leaned back in the seat next to him and accepted her drink from him.

Dan's chest was tight but he was saved from his blushes by Max charging down the stairs. He entered the room dramatically, sliding across the hardwood floor in his socks, dressed in fleecy pyjamas with his NFL shirt pulled over the top.

"Game time!"

"Nearly Maxxy."

Max jumped onto Laura's lap and started to settle himself in.

"Nope! Not a chance I'm staying to watch this, champ. I'm off to have a girls' night with your mum." Laura hoisted the boy off her lap and dumped him unceremoniously onto his uncle, before winking at them both.

Dan pulled Max into a hug and dug his fingers into the boy's side, causing him to squeal and giggle as Laura stood up from the sofa.

As she left, she snatched back Dan's bobble hat and pulled it down over her head.

"Erm, that's mine," Dan said, smiling up at her.

"Not tonight, stud. Not tonight." She sauntered out of the snug with a huge grin on her face.

By the end of the first quarter of that year's Super Bowl, as predicted, Max was fast asleep on his uncle's chest, while Dan and Martin chatted and slowly worked their way through a bottle of beer each. The boy had lasted about ten minutes into the game before the excitement of it all had gotten too much and tiredness had taken over, leaving him snuggling into his favourite uncle and drifting off to sleep.

At the quarter-time whistle, Martin had looked over. "Thought as much. I'll take him up."

"Nah, it's okay mate. I'll do it. I want to go to the loo anyway."

He carefully rose from the sofa, cradling his nephew in his arms as he did so.

"Want a drink while I'm up?" He asked.

"Yeah go on then." Martin downed the last dregs of his bottle and placed it on the floor by his feet next to Buddy, as Dan left the room.

Climbing the stairs gently, holding Max, Dan felt a contentedness he'd not felt all that often. Most of his favourite people were under one roof that night and he didn't want for anything else. While the bachelor's life was one he was happy to lead, the idea of carrying his own son to bed one day in the future, was something he knew he wanted.

He lowered his nephew onto his bed and pulled the covers over him as Max wriggled down and snuggled into his pillow, still very much asleep. Dan leant down and kissed the boy on the forehead. His heart melting, just a little bit.

As he stood and turned, he saw Laura standing in Max's bedroom doorway, smiling.

"You're adorable, you know that right?"

Dan smiled as she backed into the hall, allowing him to pull Max's bedroom door to behind him.

"He's a good kid."

"He takes after you." Laura was smiling, still sporting Dan's bobble hat. It was causing him to smile right back at her.

"You okay? We good?"

"Mhmm. We're good."

Dan pulled her into a tender hug and kissed her temple. Laura returned the affection by sliding her hands up his back.

"How's your girls' night?"

"We haven't done all that much, just talking and sharing some wine. I'm going to sleep over I think, as I don't have work in the morning."

"Makes two of us. Fancy taking Buddy for a walk tomorrow after breakfast? He'd like that."

"Mmm yeah, sounds lovely. I'd like that too."

"It's a date."

"It is?"

"Well...no...you know what I mean."

Laura chuckled into his chest, the warmth of the wine making her feel like this was the only place she wanted to be. *Were his hands stroking her back?*

"Laura?"

Pulling herself away from him slightly, she looked up. "'S'up buttercup?"

"You mean the world to me, you know that right?"

"More than Max?"

"More than Max."

"You might change your mind on that one day."

"I won't." He moved closer to her as if pulled by a force he had no control over; the hum of the game on the TV downstairs drifting up through the house.

"You promise?"

"I always keep my promises, Laura."

She looked up into his eyes, feeling her heart beating like a drum, as blood pulsed in her ears. It was like he wanted to say something, his face betraying the calmness he was trying to show.

"It's just, I want you to know...that..."

A whistle sounded from the snug, signalling the start of the second quarter and Dan's eyes flickered slightly as he was rudely pulled back into reality.

"I should get back to Martin. I was meant to get him another beer," he said, clearing his throat.

"Okay."

She felt a bit taken aback, unsure about what the fuck just happened or was about to happen as she watched him pull away and head downstairs. Her heart was racing and she desperately hoped he would change his mind and come running back up to her.

Chapter 14

The Walk

D an stirred on the sofa in the snug at Issy and Martin's house and regretted staying up to watch the game until the early hours of the morning. He wasn't sure what time it was but he knew for certain he'd not had enough sleep.

"Uncle Dan! Uncle Dan, wake up!" Max was rocking his uncle awake, not as gently as he could.

"Maxxy. What's up, mate?"

"Will you walk me to school? Please?"

Dan responded without giving the request any consideration. Anything for his nephew. "Sure thing. Just let me wake up."

Max raced away upstairs to put his school uniform on, clearly not flagging from the lack of sleep the night before.

As Dan sat up on the sofa and stretched his aching back, Buddy padded across the room and pushed his head into his owner's lap.

"Hey boy. Want to take Maxxy to school with me?" Dan said, rubbing sleep out of his eyes.

A few moments later, he was dressed and standing in the kitchen draining a cup of coffee that was too hot to drink, trying to right himself with the world.

"Come on!" Max said, dragging his godmother into the room.

"Maxxy, it's still early, little dude. Inside voice please."

"Come onnnnnn. I want you and Uncle Dan to take me to school."

Dan smiled at her as she stumbled, half asleep into the kitchen. She was wearing joggers that he assumed she'd slept in and had pulled her ever-present hoodie over her head. She had a cute look that morning which he found adorable.

"I know you do. I said I would."

When he freed her hand, so he could pick up his school bag, she pulled her hair up into a ponytail and walked over to hug Dan.

"Morning. Sleep okay?"

"Yeah as sleeping on a sofa goes, it wasn't all that bad until I was rudely awakened by the terror of the house." He smiled at his nephew.

"I didn't rudely wake you up, I was perfectly pleasant about it." Max grinned as stuffed his reading book in his bag.

Shutting the door behind them ten minutes later, the party of Dan, Laura, Max and Buddy the Border Collie walked off down the street towards Max's school, with the bright seven-year-old leading the way.

Sometimes in life, there are just moments which are one hundred percent feel good and this was one of those times. With Laura holding Buddy's lead, Dan was walking happily next to her, Max striding out in front of them; his school bag bouncing on his back with every step, making the zips jingle and jangle.

"Morning Dan. How's Max this morning?"

"He's fine thanks, Miss Stevens. He might be a little tired this morning as he stayed up to watch some of the Super Bowl with us last night but he's good."

Max looked sheepishly up as his teacher, hoping she'd not be mad at him, though she never was. He was one of those children that all teachers adored, they all said he was a joy to teach.

Dan and Laura watched him go into class but only after he'd hugged them while thanking them for bringing him to school. They both felt a sense of pride watching him walking inside with his teacher in step.

As they headed out of the school gates, Dan suggested they take the long way back so Buddy could stretch his legs a little more.

Laura slipped her arm through his. "If you want to spend more time with me Dan, you just have to say," she teased.

For a while, they walked and talked, chatting about anything and everything; letting the conversation flow easily wherever it wanted to between them.

When they reached the playing fields, Laura let Buddy off the lead and let him run, never worrying about his behaviour because Dan had trained the Border Collie so well, he would always come back on command and stay out of trouble. She tucked his lead in her coat pocket.

"Feels kind of normal doesn't it?"

"What does?" She asked.

"Walking Maxxy to school. Taking Buddy for a walk. Us. Like this."

She sighed in contentment. "Yeah, it does. Nothing ever feels quite this right."

"I know."

"It's not like this with Chris, you know?" She was speaking without thinking but didn't stop herself.

"In what way?"

"It's just not the same. Right now, I feel at peace, having dropped Max at school and watching Buddy. You're here. My heart's full, you know? When I'm with Chris like this, there's always a little bit of underlying tension and something of an agenda."

"Things not going well?"

"It's not that. They're fine. Like we aren't having troubles but…I don't know."

"It's okay if you're not okay, you know? You haven't got to put up and shut up, kid."

"No, I know. I just feel like I'm starting to realise there's no future in what I have. Chris talks about getting married and having a family and I don't know, it just doesn't feel right."

"Do you think that's because of you or him?"

Laura thought for a moment.

"A bit of both I think. He's not where I see my future and anyway, I don't think I'm ready yet."

"You'll be ready when you're ready. You'll feel it. Until then, going to that place will only end in heartache."

"What about you, Dan? You've been single for so long now. Don't you think about the future?"

"Yeah, I think about it. Of course I do. I think if you'd asked me that before Max was born, I would have told you that I wasn't considering that sort of stuff, but that kid is infectious and I dunno, there are times when I'm with him that I imagine what it would be like to have a child of my own."

Laura rested her head on Dan's shoulder as they walked slowly around the park, Buddy sniffing everything in sight ahead of them.

"You'll make a great dad. you know?"

"You're going to be a great mum. you know?"

They both smiled.

"Not yet. I'm not in the right place, I think."

"Something just feels off and you can't put your finger on it?"

"Yup. Exactly that."

"Have you talked to him about any of this?"

"No, not yet. He sees this long future ahead of us, whereas I'm just wondering when we'll all be hanging out together next and what days I'm working this week. I dunno, maybe I'm not cut out for long-term relationships. Maybe I need to be single like you."

Dan smiled and let a happy breath of air out of his nose. "It gets lonely though. Obviously, there are times when it's good, but sometimes I'd just like to be able to spend Sunday mornings tangled up in the sheets with someone I love, reading the paper and taking it slow, you know?"

Laura knew what he meant. With Chris, she didn't have those sorts of moments, even though a part of her longed for it. It just wasn't with Chris that she wanted it, although she couldn't quite explain or rationalise that feeling to herself.

"I felt like you wanted to tell me something last night? After

109

you put Max in bed." She wanted to bring him back to the night before as it had been playing on her mind.

"I did."

"Do you still want to?"

Dan sighed and slowed them to a stop.

"I just wanted to tell you that I'll always be here for you and that no matter what happens, I'll always love you. You're such an important part of my life, I don't want you to ever think that I take you or our friendship for granted."

She smiled and reached for the locket hanging around her neck.

"This," she began, "reminds me every day who you are to me. You're closer to my heart than anyone else in my life including Chris; you literally sit a few inches from my heart every minute of every day. No matter what I'm doing or what I'm going through, you're right here." She tapped the locket gently to show him.

Dan pulled her into his arms and held her close for a few happy moments.

"I'll always be here for you Laura. Always."

"I know." She replied, holding him tight. A part of her heart wished things were different and that she didn't have to hide how much she cared for him from the world. It left her with a slight feeling of guilt that she didn't want to process at that moment.

"Love you, kid."

"I know. Love you too, Dan."

*

From then on, Dan and Laura made as much time for each

other as they could. That walk and their conversation had shifted something in both of them, and they had realised, albeit somewhat unconsciously, that the friendship they shared was important and special, much more so than they had both previously believed.

Dan started making trips into town when he was working from home, just to take Laura out at lunchtime and for her part, she would regularly call him of an evening when she was walking Buddy. They just wanted to be around each other and cherish their relationship.

While all of this hadn't made Chris particularly happy, he had accepted it for the most part because he could see how it made Laura happier.

Dan and Laura's respective parents however, noticed the change in the two of them and wondered what their futures would hold. The pair had always been close friends and their families were their biggest supporters, just hoping for the best.

Chapter 15

The Talk

Dan: Hey you! You got some time at lunch today? Fancy taking a walk with me in the park?

Laura: Hey! Yeah, that'd be nice. Come meet me at the office at 12:30? X

Dan: Looking forward to it kid!

*

Standing across the road opposite the office where Laura worked, he had a horrible feeling crawling under his skin as he tried to wait patiently for her.

Their little lunchtime walks in the park were pretty normal for the pair if Dan was working from home or in town, so there was no particular reason for today to seem out of the ordinary. But today was different. He knew he just had to come out and say what needed to be said, but the wait for her to appear through the door was excruciating.

He didn't have to linger too long as, like clockwork, Laura walked out of the front door of her office building, at exactly 12:30 pm. Wearing a big smile as she often did when they met for lunch, she looked demure in white skinny jeans and a dark-coloured top, her ridiculously large sunglasses swinging in her fingertips as she crossed the road to where he waited.

Somehow, no matter the day, she always looked great. Whenever he saw her, Dan loved the ease and confidence with which she carried herself, totally at home in her curvaceous body, even though he also had to remind himself that they were only friends. Pangs of jealousy for what Chris had were haunting him more and more of late.

"Hello." She was always cute when she was in a good mood. It made his heart hurt as they hugged briefly.

"Hey, you. Work okay this morning?"

"Yeah, it's fine. Just doing some tidy-fixing on an article that's going into a corporate newsletter we've been working on. It's not really all that exciting. You?"

"Yeah, not bad. Had a video meeting this morning. That's about it so far."

"I'm surprised you're even dressed then?"

Dan chuckled. He knew that she was fully aware of his relaxed way of working at home. "Hey, I had a nice t-shirt on."

She smiled, popped her sunglasses on and linked her arm through Dan's.

"Right, come on then, let's go. I only have an hour with you today."

As they walked the short distance to the park in the warm, early summer sunshine, they caught up with the usual friend stuff but no matter how much he tried, Dan's mind was elsewhere. He treated them to '99s and led Laura to a bench, where she licked ice cream from her flake and ate it before making a start on the rest of her sweet treat. She always did that. He was going to miss those little things.

"Laura, there's something I need to tell you."

"'S'up buttercup? Laura's smile was there but underneath, instinct told her something wasn't right. They'd been friends all of her life and that kind of relationship often builds an unspoken level of communication which provides the ability to sense things before they're said.

"Erm, my meeting this morning was with a headhunter for a new coaching project."

"Okay. That's good right?" Laura knew that Dan's freelance lifestyle meant he was constantly working with different people, so projects coming and going was normal.

"Yeah, it is. It's very good for the most part."

"So...?" Sometimes you just know that the worst is yet to come and Laura hopelessly wanted to shut her eyes from what she sensed was about to hit her as she sat next to him on the park bench.

"I've been hired to work with some athletes as they prep for next year's Winter Olympics. It's mostly personal development work but it's a really big project."

"Dan, that's amazing! Congratulations!" She hugged him, careful not to cover him in sticky ice cream or to show him the worry in her eyes.

"Thanks."

"Dan. It's okay. Whatever it is, just say it. It'll be okay. Promise." She knew the bomb was yet to drop and it was turning her stomach. There was still something he wasn't telling her and she didn't care about her ice cream any more.

"It's a twelve-month contract, Laura. And it's in Montreal. I'm going to Canada."

"Oh my God! Dan, I'm so proud of you! I know you've worked really hard for an opportunity like this." She hugged him again and held him tighter this time, feeling him relax against her.

"Thanks, kid. I was really worried about telling you, and the only reason I didn't mention the meeting in advance was in case it worried you over nothing if I didn't get the contract."

"Oh, don't be silly, it's fine. I'm really happy for you." She pulled herself out of his arms and smiled through her tears.

"You sure? You're crying."

"I'm sure. They're happy tears."

"Thanks, Laura. I'm really gonna miss you, you know."

"I know. But what are you going to tell Max? He's going to be crushed."

Dan's heart broke a little as he thought about his nephew, with whom he shared a special bond. After Laura, Max was going to be the person he would miss the most.

"I dunno. I'll just tell him the truth and hope he takes it okay."

"He loves you Dan, it'll be alright. Oh! Oh! Let me organise a leaving party, you need a big send-off."

Dan was relieved that talking to Laura hadn't been as painful as he'd feared. For their whole lives, they'd been inseparable and now he was going to be away from her for twelve months but she'd taken it better than he'd thought she might.

As they joked about leaving parties and the challenges of

what to pack before he left in less than a month's time, Dan tried to visually absorb every aspect of her face. He didn't want to forget how her eyes sparkled when she was laughing or how her nose seemed to twitch when she was trying to find the right words to say about something. He watched how her lips moved, glistening with her favourite pink gloss and counted the freckles on her cheeks, watching as she blushed slightly when she looked at him. He didn't want to forget any of it.

Eventually, Laura put her hands on Dan's. "I should be getting back. I want to nip to the loo before I need to be back at my desk."

"Okay, kid. Let's get you back."

As they walked across the park to the office, Dan thanked her for her understanding. "It means a lot. After mum and dad, you're the only person who knows so far."

"Oh, don't be silly. It's fine. I'm really excited for you."

They arrived at her office door far sooner than Dan would have hoped.

"Right, give me a hug, you." She reached up and hugged his neck as she spoke.

"Call me later?"

"Yeah, after I get home, when I'm walking Buddy.

Laura didn't stay to watch him walk away, instead turned and made her way up the backstairs of the office to the toilets. Stepping into the last stall, with its broken light, locking the door, she slid to the ground and sobbed to herself in the darkness as her heart broke.

How could he leave her? He had always promised he'd be there for her. Always, he'd said. This wasn't fucking always.

The idea of twelve months without Dan in the same vicinity felt like an impossible task she didn't even want to comprehend let alone take on. Her body shook and she cried as quietly as she could, slumped in the darkness, on the tiled floor.

Her favourite person in the world. Her big brother. Her first love. Her closest friend. The one person in her life she trusted the most. The man whose face she saw every night before falling asleep.

Laura didn't care that her makeup was running down her face. Nothing seemed to be important anymore.

The main door of the toilets being opened brought her temporarily out of her misery and she pulled herself deeper into the shadows, hiding in her grief. She shrank, scared and hoping she wouldn't be found crying in the dark.

Mercifully she was alone again within a few minutes but she couldn't stay here, sitting on the toilet floor all afternoon; she knew that. So she dried her eyes on a ball of tissue paper and shaking, got to her feet, trying to compose herself as best she could. Letting out a long wobbly exhale, she pulled herself upright and unlocked the stall door.

Within five minutes, she was back at her desk, make-up retouched, no one any the wiser about her recent emotional breakdown. For the rest of the afternoon, she did what she needed to do but shut herself off from the world as she fought off wave after wave of tears. None of her colleagues had any idea anything was wrong, only that she seemed to need the toilet a little more often than usual that afternoon.

The clock seemed to tick agonisingly slower until the end

of the day.

Chapter 16

The Book

The 9:13 am train to the city rumbled its way slowly along the track, full of excited weekenders looking forward to a couple of days away from their daily routines. Sliding past the school with its empty playing fields, past The Wheatsheaf pub, desolate at this time of day, and past the shiny new supermarket recently opened by the roundabout, the four car train rattled past the back gardens of a row of old terraced houses.

In the third house along, in the living room at the back of the house, she flipped over page one of her book and took a sip of her freshly brewed coffee, deciding that it was still far too hot to drink. Her tongue felt tingly.

Her ever-faithful dog Buddy was beside her, she had the whole day to herself and she planned to spend it reading the new book she'd been given weeks before.

"It's a viral BookTok sensation babe! It's catching fire!" Sarah Miller, one of her oldest friends, had reliably informed her.

Her boyfriend was thankfully away for a couple of nights on a lads' weekend, *eye-roll,* and Laura had decided to take some time for self-care and planned to do little more than read and chill until Monday morning. With nothing more than hot drinks, Buddy and the regular rumble of trains passing at the bottom of the garden for company, she hoped to just lose herself in a book and this seemed like as good a book as any. *Every new beginning comes from some other beginning's end* piqued her interest before she even began the prologue.

"Right, boy shall we see what all the hype is about?"

Buddy lifted his chin from her thigh and sniffed in acknowledgement before settling back down in the comfort of his owner, to sleep. He had his own plans for the weekend and they all involved sleeping, eating and of course, being close to Laura.

By the time the 11:34 am lumbered past, she was hooked. Sitting in her comfies, with Buddy keeping her legs and feet warm, she rested the book in her lap and engrossed herself in the delicious words within.

*

Laura had always been a voracious reader. There was something about being totally immersed in a beautiful story that just made her happy on a basic human level. The inevitability of adult life, however, often left her going weeks without reading a single page; her latest read, retraining as a coaster sat in its now familiar spot, abandoned on the coffee table. But when she did read, she would read. A lot.

Sarah had said this new book from some unknown writer

was something special but with work being busy and no time to herself, she'd not found the time to sit and unlock its pages. Instead, *Sanctuary* had sat by her side of the sofa for weeks, unread. She'd get to it when she was ready Laura had told herself.

*

As she sat and progressed through the pages, Laura started to feel uncomfortable.

"Sorry, Buddy."

She scratched behind his ears as she adjusted her seating position for the tenth time in the last half hour and allowed him to settle down again.

To begin with, she wondered if it was this sofa that was making her uncomfortable, it had seen better days; so she'd grabbed an extra pillow and kept reading. After a while though, she decided that it wasn't the pillows at her back, so instead, she sunk down slightly and turned on her side. While she was able to read there for a while, lost in bus rides and nightmares, this position quickly became uncomfortable. So she moved. Again.

Eventually Buddy got fed up that his bed wouldn't sit still and went off to see if his bowl had filled itself.

She tried Chris's side of the sofa as she curiously read about the female main character wearing nothing but an NFL shirt and fluffy socks, which was remarkably similar to the NFL shirt Dan owned. Even though that chapter was hot, sitting on Chris's side of the sofa lasted for all of about five minutes before she marvelled at how hard and unwelcoming his side was and went back to her own.

Laura read on her front. On her back. On either side. Nothing seemed to work as she tried doggedly to read page after page. During a chapter about a Christmas ball, she even sat on the carpeted floor with her back up against the sofa cushions but that just made her bum numb, her ongoing discomfort niggling at her as she read.

"Because, whether you want to admit it or not; he isn't a friend. You love him."

Laura's skin prickled, her mind filling with images of Dan. She stared unfocused at the page in front of her, thinking about him.

It wasn't that she never thought about him, they'd been friends for a lifetime so obviously she was going to think about him a lot. And sure, okay, he was really good-looking - clearly, she was going to set him as some sort of benchmark for what attraction meant to her. That was only natural.

Maybe she shouldn't text him every day, but their friendship was important so why wouldn't she? Yes, she'd even kissed him that one time on New Year's Eve but that didn't mean anything, she was drunk and in fairness, he had looked fit. And what girl hasn't accidentally fantasised about a close male friend? Everyone did that from time to time surely?

Buddy, dreaming of chasing rabbits, whimpered in his sleep and pulled her from her thoughts. Shaking her head clear, she read on.

*

A while later, still engrossed, her phone buzzed from its resting place on the arm of the sofa.

"Shhhhh it's Christmas and he has just arrived!" She said aloud, not caring that she was talking to an inanimate object that couldn't listen and it wouldn't have stopped her even if it could. It buzzed again. Sticking her finger on the line she was reading, she picked her phone up to see who was daring to disturb her from her story. She hoped in part that it was Chris, so she could simply ignore it and carry on.

Dan: Hey you. You ok? We good? x

Laura's finger slipped from the book effortlessly as she replied to Dan with a smile on her face.

Laura: Yeah I'm good. We're good. Just reading actually. You ok? We good? x

Dan started typing as soon as her message showed as read. He often did that. She liked it.

Dan: Yeah all good. We're good. Just a friendly reminder that you said you'd pick up the balloons for my leaving do, on Wednesday night. x

She tucked a strand of hair behind her ear and snuggled into the warm embrace of the sofa and comfortable conversation with him.

Laura: Don't worry, I've not forgotten. I'm gonna pick them up for you Tuesday. I'm finishing work early and then I can bring them

123

up to the venue on Wednesday morning. x

She hit send, the words of the book still spinning through her psyche.

He wasn't a friend.

The erratic notion seemed to pound in her subconscious like a steadying heartbeat.

Dan: This is why I love you. Enjoy your book, kid x

She hated that nickname but Dan saying it always made her smile.

Laura: Love you too x

Right, where was I? Reading on, Laura was still fidgeting. She tried to re-focus and find her flow again with the words in front of her.

She'd fallen hard. She could see it now. The words that hadn't found her lips yet were rooted deeply in her heart. He had brought her back from the brink of being lost.
She looked up, tears in her eyes. "I love him."

Laura thought of Dan. *I love him.* Suddenly the source of her discomfort started to become abundantly clear.

It wasn't the sofa, or the pillows now cast on the floor, or

Buddy. It was something much deeper. As the understanding of it all settled in her mind like a puzzle taking shape, she realised that the reason she'd felt uncomfortable all day reading, was that the male lead in this book was just like Dan. Her Dan.

Her sweet and loving Dan, who always helped to save her when she needed it. Who'd only ever wanted her to be happy. And who loved her, unconditionally.

Tears formed in her eyes and for the first time all day, they had nothing to do with the book in her hands.

"My Dan," Laura said out loud, stirring Buddy who had returned to trying to sleep at her feet. He pinned his ears back and he looked at her like he knew the truth.

"Buddy. I think I'm in love with him."

If dogs could talk, Buddy would have said, *"of course, you do my dear. It's inevitable."* But instead, he just looked back happily with his cute doggy smile, just like when he was given an ice lolly in summer.

"Buddy. I'm in love with Dan. Oh my God!"

She had to stand up. A well of energy in her seemed to have been tapped and she needed to move. Pacing the living room, Laura tried to find something in the mess of emotions and thoughts in her head that she could make sense of. *Shit shit shit.*

This wasn't how she had planned to spend her weekend but walking circles around the coffee table, everything just seemed to make sense. *Fuck!* Dan had been her first crush, her closest friend and apparently the love of her fucking life. *Shit!*

Buddy watched her freaking out and again, had he been

able to talk would have said, *"How did you not know? We've all known for ages!"* But dogs can't talk, so he left her to work it out alone.

Glancing across the room, her eyes fell onto the bookshelf in the corner of the room; a picture of Dan with his big sister Issy and their parents, poised next to a matching one of Laura with her parents, both photos taken on a shared holiday. Her gaze was drawn to the man smiling at the back of the Muir family photo. Her Dan.

But as she smiled back at him from across the room, Laura's eyes fell onto another picture on the shelf, off to the side, hidden behind a postcard from her parents. A photo of her and Chris. Her heart sank a little. *Fuck! What am I going to do?* Even looking at them there, immortalised forever in 6x5 lustre print, she realised how wrong they looked together.

Sitting back on the sofa, she stared off into nothingness for a moment, unable to think straight. Her whole life, she'd spent time in the company of someone she'd always just assumed was a friend. Someone she had often looked at but clearly never seen.

But he'd become so much more without her realising fully and now reading this fucking book, she was sure. It had only ever been Dan.

Buddy whined and put his paw on the now discarded copy of *Sanctuary*. Dogs just know, don't they?

Laura pulled it gently from under his claws and sat back, bringing her legs up and crossing them in front of her. And for the first time that day, with the 4:57 pm train taking the last of the evening revellers into the city, she finally found a comfortable spot and smiled to herself amidst all the confusion.

"Shall we see if they get their happy ending Buddy?

As her faithful Border Collie rested his head in her lap once more, Laura Gray read on to discover that they did in fact get a happy ending, while hoping against hope that there was one for her, in her future.

Chapter 17

The Rebound

"You okay Laura?"

She stood on Issy's doorstep at 3:00 pm on a warm Sunday afternoon, looking like she needed a friend.

"Martin!" Issy shouted over her shoulder. "I'm outside with Laura, I'll be back in a little while! Make sure Max finishes his homework!"

Shutting the large white door behind her with a comforting thud, she led Laura down the path that wound through her front garden and sat her on the vintage wrought iron bench.

"Sorry Issy, I know it's family time and stuff. I just needed a friend."

"Don't be silly! Martin's just watching the NFL game and Max is sitting with him supposedly doing some homework." She waved back at her husband who was waving, perplexed but not concerned, through the window of the snug. "They'll be fine for a few minutes and I need a break from sports! What's up?"

Laura wrung her hands together and looked at her feet.

"I think me and Chris are over."

"Okay."

"You don't seem surprised."

"I'm not."

She wasn't. Issy had always felt like Laura and her long term boyfriend Chris wouldn't last the distance. "What makes you think you two are over?"

"I read a book yesterday."

"That's always dangerous, although don't tell Max I told you that. I'd love to see him read anything but his phone."

Laura seemed like she was in a muddle, Issy could tell, so she left the jokes for a moment. "What book did you read?"

"It's called *Sanctuary*. It's a love story about two people who fall in love even though it seems impossible. The lead male character…"

"Is a bit like Dan?" Issy cut her younger friend off. She'd read this particular book soon after it had been released and had loved it from start to finish. She knew exactly what Laura was thinking; the main male character was very much like Dan in so many ways, although her brother had the ability to make it look like any photo he'd taken, he'd used a microwave in a dark room, and not a camera.

"Yeah, a lot like Dan."

"Well it's not uncommon for characters in stories to seem like people we know and love."

"Issy. Cut the crap. Please."

The older woman smiled. She had been trying to not engage with where Laura was taking this conversation, in the hope that she would just come out and say whatever was on her mind.

"Okay. So let me see if I understand this right. Reading this book has made you realise that you're actually in love with my baby brother and not Chris. Now you're sure that you need to end things with Chris because you don't truly love him but you're panicking because Dan's going away in a few day's times and you're worried you'll miss your chance."

"Yeah that's about it. What the fuck do I do?"

Issy looked out over her front garden in the afternoon sun. "I know what happened that New Years Eve you know? When you first went to uni."

"I thought you might. It was a mistake, Issy. I was a bit tipsy and looking for a connection."

"If I'm cutting the crap, do me a favour and cut your own." She gently nudged Laura. "He told me the following morning. He was really panicky that you'd be upset and feel rejected by it all and that was the last thing he wanted."

"I did feel rejected." Laura could still feel the hurt and confusion of that night like it was yesterday, lingering deep inside her.

"Oh, I know you did. That's why you ended up with Chris."

"I...what?" Laura could feel Issy's eyes on her as she flustered with her words, trying to hide the secret she'd known in part was true for the last few years.

"Look, Chris is a nice guy and you two would probably have a cute little life together but he is and always will be the rebound from being rejected by Dan."

The words hung heavy in the air as Issy continued.

"Now listen, Dan's an idiot – he's my idiot, but he's still an idiot. However, he did do the right thing that night. You were too young back then to get into a relationship with an older guy. It takes a certain level of maturity and understanding of yourself to be with someone who is ten years older than you and back then you had neither.

You did the natural thing; you found someone your own age who wouldn't reject you and made you feel good. The only problem with that solution is, you've ended up with him for the last nine years."

Laura knew it was true. She had always known on some level that Chris had been there in the right place, at the right time when she needed some attention after the Christmas break of her first year of university.

"But it's always been Dan, hasn't it?" Issy continued, "that kind of love doesn't really go away."

Laura nodded, more to herself than as a confirmation to the woman sitting next to her. "It's always been Dan I think. Deep down I guess I've always known but reading this fucking book has made it obvious and now I can't hide from it."

Issy chuckled.

"What?" Laura asked, confused.

"You really do have the worst timing, don't you?"

"Yeah, seems that way. Jesus Issy, what am I going to do?"

"Okay, well the way I see it you have two problems which in my mind need to be treated separately." Issy paused but when no objections were given, she carried on. "You need to end things with Chris really. It's only fair to both of you. And then you need to decide what to do about Dan."

"Why is it that I feel like breaking up with Chris is going to be the easy bit?"

"Probably because on the surface, it is. Look, he's a nice guy don't get me wrong, but you're not in love with him. And that's okay. But now it's time to free him from that and deal with who you do love."

"I'm scared, Issy."

"Of what?"

"Of being with Dan. Ten years is a big difference in age."

"It is for sure, but Martin is eight years older than me, and he might annoy me constantly, but I've been in love with him since the first time he kissed me and nothing will ever change that."

"I'm not sure I fell in love with Dan that night. All I recall is that I wanted to kiss him."

"Oh, it's been much longer than that Laura! You've been in love with my brother for as long as I can remember. There's just something about you two when you're together. It's not obvious, I mean you're not drooling over him whenever he's around, but I can see it in your eyes."

"What would you do about Dan? If you were me?"

"I'd tell him."

Laura looked painfully across the garden and wished she could just stay here, avoiding her problems forever.

"Feel the fear and do it anyway, Laura."

"Isn't that what your dad used to tell us?"

"That's the one."

Laura sighed as she tried to accept what she needed to do.

"You're in love with Dan. You know it. I know it. Now you just need to decide when he needs to know it."

"I don't think I can tell him before he goes, Issy. That's no way to say goodbye to someone."

"Yeah, true but if you leave it, you run the risk of it consuming you for a year which isn't going to be nice for you or worse, we end up with another Chloe situation."

Both women shuddered simultaneously and then laughed together.

"She really was something else, wasn't she."

"Yup! She was." Laura smiled in agreement but the shadow Dan's plus-one cast on her self-confidence was still there in a small way.

Issy sensed what her friend was thinking and took her hand in her own.

"She wasn't his type anyway, don't worry. I suspect Dan has always preferred curvy blondes."

"Oh?" She cast Issy a questioning look. "Is that right?"

"Mhmm, but don't quote me on that just yet."

A cheer went up from the snug and Issy sighed.

"Great. Some guy has scored a touchdown and now everyone is praising him." She shrugged at a game she didn't understand. "I should get back in though otherwise, Max will never actually finish his homework.

The women stood and walked back up along the gravel path.

"Thanks Issy. Really. For everything."

"It's okay. You know what you need to do Laura. We all love you and will always support you."

At the front door, as she watched Laura driving away, Issy sighed

"All okay?"

Issy turned to see her husband, Martin, stood in the doorway to the snug and gave him a confused look.

"Half time," he explained without being asked.

Her shoulders sank a little as she relaxed. "Yeah all okay. Just what we always knew would happen is starting to happen."

"Ah." This wasn't a particular surprise to him. "Is she okay? Should I message Dan?"

"No. This is for them to handle, we just need to let them sort it. And yes, Laura's fine, just a bit shell-shocked and muddled up over it."

"I mean that's understandable. You sure you don't want me to go for a drink with Dan and talk to him?"

Martin and Dan had been best friends for over ten years, so Issy knew her husband had good intentions.

"No, it's fine. This is something they need to do alone. Just keep your phone on loud for a bit while this all plays out. He might need you."

A whistle from the 56" TV in the room to their left blew. Martin looked pained.

"Go," she said ruefully, shaking her head with a smile.

"Love ya, babe!"

"Yeah yeah. Love you too."

Martin returned to their son and the game while Issy wandered, lost in thought down the hall to the kitchen. She needed a brew.

"Max! Homework!" She shouted as she flicked the kettle on, to the groan of the boys in the other room.

Chapter 18

The Dress

Sarah pulled up in the car park to see Laura waiting by the pay machines at the entrance. She didn't feel like this afternoon would just be about party supplies, having given Laura a copy of *Sanctuary* to read a few weeks before. She knew her friend couldn't resist reading something good but Laura had been pretty quiet about it since.

The girls hugged hello and Sarah couldn't help but feel like her friend seemed lighter in spirit. Something about her was different although it wasn't readily apparent from their simple interaction. Sarah frowned.

"What?" Laura looked slightly taken aback.

"You. You're different somehow."

"No, I don't think so. I'm just regular old me."

Sarah wasn't buying it. Something was different.

"Right, shall we go get these balloons then and you can keep up the pretence a while longer?"

Laura grinned. "Sounds good!"

They spent an hour or so going around town with fellow early evening shoppers, collecting the necessary supplies for Dan's leaving party. As chief party liaison (self-appointed), Laura knew all the things they needed to get and had planned out the order in which they were going to collect them.

A card from the stationers, big enough for everyone important to him to sign during the evening. She'd picked a nice one but decided that the cute one she'd picked out for herself to give him personally was nicer still. That made her happy.

The pub was sorting the catering out, so all they needed to do was pick up the cake, which Laura had preordered from the bakery. It was a block of iced sponge cake decorated to make it look like a runway and on top sat a fondant cartoon jumbo jet, taking off. Laura was pleased with that one as she'd designed it herself and although she couldn't really draw what she wanted, she had had an in-depth discussion with the baker who had created exactly what she'd imagined.

Next, with Sarah in tow carrying the cake in a large white box, they went to pick out Laura's outfit for the evening. It wasn't a dress-up event particularly, so she went on the hunt for a nice sundress.

After a few minutes of running her fingers along clothing racks, she found one that she felt might work and went to try it on.

"Interesting choice," Sarah remarked as she saw Laura twirling in the mirror outside the changing room.

"What does that mean?"

"Oh, only that you look like you're going on a date rather than saying goodbye to one of your oldest friends."

Laura looked at herself in the mirror and knew she had

found the one. The cornflower blue dress was really pretty. The floaty material, covered in a small, white ditsy print, sat gently on her body but had been stitched to pinch in beneath her bust and over her hips, giving the dress a curvy outline which flowed out into easy ruffles over her thighs. Thin straps held it up, running over her shoulders, crisscrossing between her shoulder blades, meeting the back of the dress in the small of her back. It floated as she spun in her white pumps. It was perfect.

"I just want to look nice Sarah, that's all."

"Sure you do." Sarah couldn't help but smile.

As they walked to the party shop to collect the balloons which would float by the main table at the party, Sarah had had enough of waiting for Laura to spill the beans and decided some gentle prodding was in order.

"So you're planning on looking good for him tomorrow then?"

"Chris? No, not really. I just want to look nice."

"For Dan, I mean."

"Erm I mean it's a big night and of course I want to look good."

"And this shopping for all these things?"

"I'm just trying to be helpful, that's all. He's got loads to do before he flies."

"Right. Right. Got it."

Sarah changed tack.

"By the way, did you get to read the book I lent you?"

Laura paused for a moment which her best friend picked up on.

"It was erm…good, yeah."

"How did you feel reading it?"

"Feel? What do you mean?"

"I mean how did it make you feel, Laura?"

"It was a beautiful story."

"Right. Okay."

It was Laura's turn to voice the question she'd been dying to ask all afternoon.

"Sarah? Did that lead male character remind you of anyone?"

"I don't know what you mean, Laura."

Sarah stopped walking, causing Laura to turn and look back. They looked at each other for a moment, no words spoken but everything was said in the look they exchanged. Resting the cake gently on her lap, Sarah sat down on a nearby bench.

"Are you going to tell him?"

"I haven't decided what I'm going to do yet," she said, casting her eyes downwards a little.

"But you are…?"

"Mhmmm, head over heels in love with him. Yup." There was no shame in her words.

Sarah smiled.

"How long have you known?" Laura asked.

"Since you were thirteen and he came to your birthday party. Remember? We all went to your bowling party, where the casino is now, and he turned up with that massive present for you all wrapped up with ribbons and bows. I knew then. Back then it was easy for us as kids to say we loved or fancied someone but the look in your eyes as he sat with you and you opened his gift? I've seen that look in your eyes every time you've been around each other since. It's never left you."

As she thought back to her life with Dan, Laura knew what her friend was saying was true. It was around that time that her crush on him had really become apparent even though she hadn't told anyone. He was older and she worried about what people would say and it confused her too as he was like family. As she'd gotten older the crush had remained, though her life had moved on and casual boyfriends her own age had come and gone until eventually Chris, her first serious boyfriend had stuck and she'd settled into her life with him. But the thought of Dan and her feelings for him still lingered deep in her soul, like a comfy chair you just keep going back to because it just feels right.

Reading *Sanctuary* had brought that crush right back to the forefront of her heart and the maturity and experience that comes with age told her it wasn't simply a crush any more. It was love. Proper, romance book and Netflix movie love.

"This could get really messy, Sarah."

Her friend nodded in sympathy. "I know. The fallout could be big. If you two ever got together, do you think your families would be okay with it?"

Laura moved to sit next to her friend. "I dunno. Maybe. They've never shown any concern about how close we are. But this is different."

"Would you go to Canada to see him?"

"Probably. I don't think I could go a whole year without seeing him if we were together as a couple. But then there's Buddy to think about it."

"And you're sure this isn't just because you're scared he's going away?"

"No. I thought about that a lot over the weekend. I am

scared he's going away. But that's *because* I love him and not because of anything else. I'm scared of losing him because of how I feel."

"Have you wondered how he feels? About you?"

"Yeah. I can't make my mind up on that. A part of me thinks it's just me who feels this way, that I've read the signs wrong and lost myself in how I feel about him. That's scary for sure. But then when I think about things, I also wonder if he does like me too. We're so close. Sometimes he looks at me in a way that makes me wonder if he's going to kiss me or if there's something being left unsaid. I dunno Sarah. If he likes me too, that feels even scarier. Could I ever live up to his expectations?"

"Babe, if he likes you in the same way, you already meet his expectations.Dan's not the kind of guy to want you to be or to act a certain way. If he likes you, then he likes you for you as you are and not some perceived way you could be for him."

"Yeah, I guess." Laura felt lost in thought at all the permutations of what now might happen.

"There is one thing we haven't talked about yet."

"Yeah, I was kinda hoping we could just skip over that bit."

"You'll need to deal with Chris, one way or the other Laura. You know it's the right thing to do."

"I know. He doesn't deserve this, I know that much."

"So the question then becomes when do you tell Dan?"

Laura didn't have an answer. It was all still unclear in her mind. If she told Dan before he left, what if that changed his plans? She couldn't do that to him, he'd worked so hard to get himself into a position where this kind of opportunity was a reality for him. But if she didn't tell him, he might meet someone while he was away and the horrific idea of him staying out there, in love with someone else was just too hard to comprehend.

She stood up and forced a smile onto her face. "Not today. We have balloons to get."

Her friend stood too and as they walked to the party supply shop, Sarah knew that the day would come soon when all of their questions would be answered one way or another.

Chapter 19

The Declaration

L aura looked across the bar and realised she was fucked. No matter what happened now, in her life or in her relationship with Chris, she knew that Dan had her heart. It wasn't some stupid crush; she'd made her mind up on that. It was deeper than a crush and she knew that accepting that she loved him, meant she could never come back from it. He put the colours into her world.

Dan hadn't stolen her heart. He'd not even tried. He was just there. And her heart had leapt to him as if by some cosmic attraction; a pull she had no control over or will to fight. She knew he was the second half of her heart.

She'd been fighting internally for days, trying to work out what was best. Tonight, she'd arrived having decided to just leave it and talk to him when he returned in a year's time. But walking in and seeing him there in his favourite NFL jersey, looking stupidly wonderful, she knew she couldn't do it. He was her everything.

What the fuck do I do now?

*

She felt for Chris. He wasn't a bad guy. He just wasn't Dan. And nothing could change that. She'd sentenced herself to life by admitting that she was in love with Dan. And there was nothing she could do or wanted to do to change it.

For so long she'd been content enough with Chris; she'd settled into a nice easy life, house and vague future plans, she hadn't wanted for anything on the surface. And yet there had always seemed to be something missing which she'd never been able to put the right label on. Now, staring at Dan across the bar watching him smile and laugh with those around him, she understood. Dan was that label.

*

Sarah tapped her on the shoulder, making her jump out of her skin.

"Fuck sake Sarah!"

The taller girl smiled. "Penny for your thoughts?"

Laura looked back over at Dan, as the din of the busy bar rumbled around her and her heart sank.

"Sarah, what the fuck do I do?"

Letting her eyes slide from her friend, across the room to Dan with his familiar salt and pepper hair, Sarah knew that the time had finally come for Laura to face her daemons. "Tell him."

"What if he rejects me? What if he stays for me? What if it makes a massive scene at his leaving party?"

"Look," Sarah began, "the way I see it is this - if you tell him, Dan's not the type to end your friendship if he doesn't feel the same way. If he says thanks but no thanks, then you smile and carry on your life with Chris, unless that has gone past the point of no return. If he feels the same way then, yeah we have some problems ahead of us but I think here logic dictates that you tell him how you feel. He leaves in the morning for twelve months. You might not get this chance again babe."

"Fuck sake." Laura's heart sunk a little further but she knew her friend right. He was leaving to work in Canada and would be gone for a year; by the time he returned, everything could have changed.

Even though her world was lurching like a rollercoaster, Laura knew that she had to act now. Dan had always told her to feel the fear and do it anyway, and that advice had served her well to date.

*

The evening had been lovely.

Between the two families and with added help from Sarah, they'd set up the function room in the pub and made it look really special; the balloons looking majestic behind the buffet table. Even though it wasn't a surprise, Dan had been taken aback when he'd walked in and saw the effort that had been made on his behalf.

Hugging Laura as he thanked her, he couldn't help but notice how incredible she looked in, what he could only assume was a new blue sundress. He would definitely have remembered if he had seen her wear this previously.

"Thank you. This is amazing." He said, breathing in the vanilla of her perfume. He was going to miss that smell.

"You're very welcome. Couldn't send you off with just a pint and a packet of scampi fries could we?"

Throughout the party, Laura flipped between the two different sides of her decision as she watched Dan enjoying the company of those people who mattered the most to him in the world. It made her happy and sad in equal measure.

Chris had even made a concerted effort to be supportive as he knew she was finding it hard to say goodbye to her best friend. While she knew he still didn't particularly like Dan, Laura realised that Chris had at least come to terms with it all now, even though it had taken him years to do so. Little did he know that their time was up and she was about to break his heart.

By the end of the evening, Laura knew there was only one way out of this situation and even Sarah had confirmed it.

*

As if directed by some higher power, Dan left his conversational group and appeared in front of her with a big smile on his face.

"Hey, you," he said looking down into her eyes.

Fuck! It was now or never.

"Hey, you," she said, smiling back.

"Nearly time for me to go, kid."

"I know. Can we go talk somewhere for a minute before you do?"

Dan cocked his head to the side. "You okay? We good?"

"All good, just want to talk to you about something."

Laura's heart was in her throat but curiously she didn't feel scared. What she was feeling, as they walked out of the bar together into the fresh evening air of the outside patio, was an inevitability. Like when you know you're going to crash into something and there's no point in trying to avoid it; it's going to happen anyway, better to just brace for it and absorb the impact. Laura was about to crash into Dan so hard it was going to leave an indelible mark on the universe.

"What's up?" He looked slightly concerned but knew Laura well enough to know she would say what she needed to say. They'd always had that kind of friendship, having grown up together, telling one another whatever was on their mind.

"Where do I start?" It was something of a rhetorical question and one she didn't know the answer to herself.

Dan took her hand in his and caught her gaze, "hey, it's me. You can talk to me about anything. Okay? Deep breath and start at the beginning."

As she looked back at him, trying to find the words, all she wanted to do was fall with him through time and space, never letting go. "Just promise me you won't hate me?"

"Whoa! That's not gonna happen. Ever!" Dan pulled her into a hug. He'd always kept her safe throughout their entire lives together, from bumped knees to broken hearts, he'd been there for her and she loved him for it.

"I love you," she said it softly, but loud enough for him to hear. She was resigned to her fate now, this had to happen regardless of how it played out.

"I love you too, Laura," he replied instinctively, as he always did whenever she told him she loved him.

146

"No, Dan." She sighed. "I love you." She kept her face turned against him so she didn't have to look up into his blue eyes. "I'm in love with you. I think I always have been."

Resting his chin gently on the top of her head, Dan let out a breath. He knew what she was saying; this wasn't a casual *I love you* good friends thing. "Laura, that's a big thing to say."

"I know, but it's the truth."

She pulled herself away from his embrace reluctantly and sat on one of the low planters nearby, holding her head in her hands. "I know how fucked up this is. Trust me, I know. I know I'm with Chris. I know you're going away. I know we've been just like brother and sister for years. I know. Jesus, I know. Dan." She was trembling, trying to not lose the plot.

Standing where she'd left him, Dan looked at her. She was everything he could ever want in life. While he'd spent a lifetime being the big brother she'd never had, he was fully aware that in recent years, he'd developed something of a crush on her. He'd watched her go from freckly, awkward kid to beautiful woman and she'd left him breathless on more than one occasion in recent years, seemingly without even trying. Seeing her tonight in that beautiful blue sundress had been yet another one of those times.

But this wasn't just a throwaway comment between friends; this was serious and the implications could fuck up a lot of things. He knew that only too well.

Moving to crouch in front of her, Dan gently placed his hand on her leg just above her knee, stroking his thumb on her soft skin to reassure her that he was there. "Laura, are you saying you don't want to be with Chris anymore?"

She let out a shuddering breath.

"I'm saying that the only man I want to be with is you, Dan."

He felt his world shift and all of a sudden, accepting a coaching job in Canada seemed like a fucking stupid idea. He also knew that there was a high chance Laura was just confused about her feelings and that if he was to jump at the chance sitting in front of him, a lot could go south at a frightening pace.

The logical part of his brain engaged long enough to see some sense in the situation, even though his heart broke a little to speak the words.

"Laura, that's a lot but here's the thing; if you want to be with me, you clearly don't want to be with Chris and while that's fine, you need to sort that and work out what happens next for you. You know I'll love and support you in whatever you decide. But you also need time; I don't want to be some easy rebound while you figure out if you've made a mistake or not.

I'm leaving in the morning. We've got a whole year apart now but we'll stay in touch like we always do. I'm not going anywhere I promise, and when I get back we can talk again. I will think about what you've said but I need some time too. If this is what you truly want though, we can't rush into it. I'm not gonna be the guy who comes between two people and possibly ruins two families in the process. I can't."

Laura felt a tear roll down the side of her nose and drip onto the ground below her. He was right. She needed to do some big things now that didn't involve him at all but she hoped to hell that when Dan came back in a year, she still stood a chance.

"I'm sorry Dan." More wet spots hit the ground beneath he, building into a small pool of emotion on the concrete at her feet. "I can't help how I feel."

Dan kissed her head and kept up the tender touch on her leg. "You have nothing to say sorry for." Adding gently, "I've only ever wanted you to be happy, you know that. If this is how you feel that's okay. I just want you to do this the right way."

Nodding, she sniffed away more tears.

"I should go though. It's nearly time for me to head home and get some sleep before my flight in the morning. I'm sorry. I really am." Dan Muir never wanted to leave anyone less in his life.

"Yeah, okay," she replied, defeated. They both stood up, Laura feeling awkward in front of him for the first time in her life.

Sensing her building discomfort, just like he always seemed able to do, as though he could read her mind, Dan sighed and smiled. "It'll be okay. Don't worry. I'm not running away."

"No, you're getting on a plane for seven fucking hours." Wrapping her arms around him, Laura tried to make light of it. Even though she'd just declared her love for him, she realised that he still held her the same; he wasn't holding back because he knew her feelings and she loved him more for that.

"You okay? We good?" She asked.

"We're good. Promise." Holding her close Dan felt certain that his life had just changed irrevocably. He just wasn't sure yet if it was for the better or not, as he felt her warmth melting into him. "I gotta go. But please message me. I don't want us to not talk for days."

Squeezing him harder for a moment, she accepted her fate. "I'll do what I need to do. Thank you for not hating me."

"There's nothing you can do that would ever make me hate you, Laura. Nothing in the world."

"Can I message you tomorrow? Please?" She asked knowing he'd not say no but wanting to ask anyway. She needed that confirmation that he wanted her continued presence in his life.

"Of course. Say hi whenever. If I'm in the air, I'll reply when I touch down. Promise."

And with that, Dan slid away and walked back into the bar to say his goodbyes to the family and friends who'd come out to wish him well.

*

Dave spotted his daughter through the full-length glass patio doors, sitting by herself on the reused railway sleepers that made up the decorative flower beds in the outside area of the bar. She looked lost, like the weight of the world was on her shoulders and she had no way of knowing how to handle it. But having been Laura's father for twenty-seven years, he knew what was weighing down on her and he fully understood what she would now need to do.

His heart broke for her but he knew what she was about to set in motion was how it was meant to be.

*

"You okay baby?" Chris Jones asked, quietly shutting the patio door behind him. "Saw you saying goodbye to Dan. You okay?"

Laura's long-term boyfriend had no idea of the storm that was about to engulf and drown him.

"Yeah. Can we just go home please?" She rose and made her way past him.

"Laura? What's wrong?" He knew something wasn't right but having never been able to fully get in his girlfriend's head, he didn't really seem to know what was happening.

Turning to him and taking his hand, in a false gesture that made her feel slimy, she smiled up at him. "I'm tired Chris, that's all. Let's just go okay?"

Chapter 20

The Break Up

"What do you mean you don't want to be with me anymore? We have a life together."

He was in shock. Actually, shock didn't quite cut it; what Chris Jones felt as Laura sat in front of him with a look of shame on her face, was that his life was in complete and utter freefall.

"Chris, I'm so sorry." She had delivered the news less than a minute before even though she'd felt sick to her stomach.

*

Coming home from Dan's leaving party, Laura sat quietly in the car as Chris drove, completely unaware of the world of devastation about to befall him. She knew that it had to be done and it had to be done tonight; anything else would be unfair to him.

Yes, she could have waited till the morning but her confidence might have faltered after a night's sleep and anyway, tomorrow she didn't want to think about having to end her relationship while also trying not to think about Dan boarding his flight and leaving her for a year.

It needed to happen tonight. There was no other way.

She watched the night slipping past her through the passenger window of Chris's Golf GTi, absentmindedly looking for plane lights in the sky above her and thought about what she needed to do. As she looked up, the sky was clear and she could make out the different constellations of stars she'd learned about as a kid. A part of her knew that even when Dan would be thousands of miles away, there'd be times when they'd be looking at the same stars. Together.

Laura appreciated that the easy decision was to end things with Chris. Regardless of her tangled-up feelings for Dan, she was fully aware that she could no longer be in any kind of relationship with her boyfriend; her heart just wasn't in it anymore, if it ever truly was. She loved Chris in her own way, even though she wasn't in love with him; he deserved the truth and to be allowed to be set free from the prison they'd built for themselves.

As she lost herself quietly in her thoughts, she realised that her life was something she'd settled for rather than worked to create. Her nice little home, her comfortable job working as a copywriter for a local ad agency in the town where she'd grown up, her hobbies, her boyfriend. She'd settled for everything.

The only time she'd felt any sense of what her heart truly desired, was when she spent time with Dan. Her pulse fluttered just saying his name in her head.

153

As her mind whirled with a million variations of how to say *it's over,* Laura looked over at Chris who was focused on the dark road ahead of him, completely unaware that the dangers that threatened his safety lay at home, not in the ten feet of tarmac illuminated by the Golf's headlights.

*

Having sat Chris down at their small dining table in the 3-bed terrace house they rented together; Laura hadn't waited as he could tell something was up.

"You okay baby? We good?" He'd asked.

What the fuck is he playing at? She knew for certain then and there, what she was about to do was the right decision.

She knew the longer she tiptoed around it the harder this whole sorry situation would be. She needed to rip off the Bandaid.

"What do you mean you don't want to be with me anymore? We have a life together."

"Chris, I'm so sorry. But I don't want this anymore and it's unfair to you for me to stay if I know it's not what I want. You are a wonderful guy and you deserve every happiness in this world, but I'm not the one to give it to you." Her calmness as she spoke surprised both of them.

"Laura, I love you. Can't you stay and we can fix this? This isn't fair. I didn't know there was a problem!" He shook with every word. His whole world was coming down around him, smashing into pieces that seemed to ricochet off one another causing more destruction to the life he'd built.

Sitting with him, wanting to hold his hand but knowing it wasn't the right gesture, Laura watched his heart breaking. "I

154

can't Chris. I'm sorry. I know this is hard but I know in my heart that I can't stay."

His head hurt. He felt sick. He didn't understand.

*

They had a good life together. After meeting in the first year of uni, they'd settled into a comfortable easy relationship together and had been happy. He felt like he'd found the girl he could settle down with for life. Rather than moving back home, they felt like getting a house together was the next logical step when they'd completed their degrees. So a few years later, they moved into a nice terraced house on the other side of town from Laura's parents and even brought her dog, Buddy, back to live with them.

For some reason, she'd always ducked the topic of marriage and kids but he put it down to them being young and wanting to make the most of their freedom. In fairness to Laura, she didn't really know the reason for that, but talk of the future was scary and she'd done well for the length of their nine-year relationship, to avoid in-depth conversations about how Chris viewed their future.

Chris and Laura were just a given. No one could ever say they were made for each other but seeing them together, out with friends or family, they just seemed to go comfortably together, like bread and butter.

*

"Can I at least know why?" He needed some sort of vague logic to cling to.

Laura sighed. The right thing to do would be to tell him the whole truth; that it was Dan who she *knew* she belonged with, but knowing and doing are two different things and so all she could say was, "it's for the best, Chris."

"That's not a fucking answer, Laura." He wasn't mad, but the hurt in his face was portraying the pain in his heart as his mind reeled trying to piece together what had gone wrong.

"I'm just not happy Chris. I know you think this can be fixed but it can't."

"At least let me try."

"Chris. No."

"Did I break this? Did I break us?"

"No." She was struggling to hold eye contact.

"Is it Dan?"

"No Chris. Please."

"Really? Cos there's been three people in this relationship for the whole time, and I'm fucked if I believe he doesn't have something to do with this."

"This is on me, Chris. This is my choice. Dan doesn't know." She felt awful for lying.

"Is there someone else?"

"No!" She knew he had to ask but still. *Fuck.*

"Then why am I being punished for something I didn't break?"

"Chris, please. Understand this, this isn't anything you've done or not done. There's no-one at fault here."

"So that's it?"

"Yeah." Unsure of what to say next without wanting to break down in front of her, Chris got practical.

"So what happens now?"

Laura already knew what her next steps were and she hated

herself for it.

"You stay here tonight. I'll go to Mum and Dad's." She didn't want to finish that sentence because she knew what she was about to do would hurt her more than what had already gone before.

As if on cue, Buddy whined from his bed in the corner of the room causing Laura to shed tears for the first time since being home.

Chris laughed a little through his nose, but there was no merriment in it.

"Just leave him here. I'll do his walks and stuff. We can figure out what happens with him later."

"Thank you."

"Right. Do you need time to get some things?"

The finality in his voice shocked her slightly but at least they weren't slinging verbal blows across the dining room table, waking the neighbours.

"Erm, yeah. Just let me grab a few bits and then I'll go."

"Fine." Chris got up and went into the kitchen, in some kind of stupid display of macho control on the situation he didn't have any grasp of. Laura nodded to herself sitting at the table alone, relieved it was over before rising and going to the bedroom.

*

As she packed some things into a bag, she realised that it didn't hurt. A part of her thought that leaving would be hard; not leaving Chris but leaving her home. Tellingly, she just didn't care about not being in this room again as she placed the last remaining things in her bag.

Walking down the stairs she found Chris waiting in the hall below.

"Got everything you want?"

"Yeah, I think so."

"Right."

Laura knew she just needed to go out of the front door and it would be over.

"Well, if you have everything you *want* now," he continued, "I'm going to bed." Brushing past, he left her standing on her own in the hallway. The same hallway she'd come home into every day since they moved in together. Hearing the bedroom door shut, she sighed.

It was done. It was over.

Buddy's wet nose found her hand as it hung by her side.

"Oh, Buddy."

He knew. Dogs just know, don't they?

She sat herself down on the bottom step of the stairs and held his face in her hands, tears running down her cheeks.

"I have to go. I'm so sorry."

Buddy just stared back looking into her eyes.

"You stay here for a day or two. Let me get settled. I'll be back for you Buddy, I promise. I want you to be safe while everything else is broken. And you can't go to Dan because… he's not here."

She sobbed her heart out, not holding back her emotions or even trying to stop herself.

"I'll come back for you," she whispered as she rested her head on his, "I promise."

*

Turning the corner of the street in her car, Laura let the tears of leaving Buddy behind fall freely again. It had been harder than she'd imagined it would be. Whenever she'd left Buddy with Dan, it had never felt this bad, even if she was leaving him for a few months to go back to uni. This feeling was another level of pain. But she was resolved to get him back, and soon.

She realised that while she knew she would be staying at her parents' tonight, she hadn't actually asked them, let alone explained what had happened. Pulling over into an empty bus stop in the dark, she called her dad.

Dave Gray picked up on the second ring.

"You okay, Muffin? What's up?"

"Me and Chris are over." She didn't know what else to say, painfully aware that her parents might be disappointed.

"Ah, baby girl. Come home."

"Thanks, Dad." She sobbed, not from the breakup but from a vile collection of emotions that had built up upon themselves, during the last few hours.

"You okay? Do you need me to come and get you?"

"No, it's okay Dad. I'm already on my way. Be there in a bit."

Hanging up the phone, she drove out of the bus stop and carried on to her parents' house, wondering what her life would be like now. She wondered if she should message Dan, but guessed he'd probably be asleep already, bags packed at the foot of his bed ready to head to the airport in the morning. The irony that they were both leaving home at the same time whilst being pulled thousands of miles apart wasn't lost on her. But at least now, the path was clear for her to get ready for Dan when he came back home.

159

Chapter 21

The Sibling Plan

Dan shut the boot of his sister's car, securing his suitcase and carry-on, and went to check he'd locked the front door for the fifth time. Issy sat in the driver's seat with the engine running, skipping through the radio stations trying to find something mildly inoffensive for this time of the morning. Two hot cups of coffee sat in their holders in the centre console; she'd picked them up from the drive-thru on the way to collect her brother that morning.

"All good I think. Although I feel like I'm leaving something at home that I shouldn't?" He checked his pockets for the essentials one more time as he climbed into the passenger seat. "Let's go. Anything I've forgotten now, I'm just going to have to live without for a bit."

Issy pulled out onto the street and let Dan gather his thoughts. She couldn't imagine the inner turmoil he was going through at that precise moment; a mixture of excitement for the year ahead with a side dish of fear and trepidation for leaving everything and everyone at home behind him.

She was proud of him for everything he'd achieved with his business over the past few years, turning his love of sport and helping people into a thriving coaching business that helped countless athletes around the world to perform at their best.

While he would always be on the end of a phone whenever she wanted him, she knew she'd miss him. Dan was a very regular visitor at her family home, spending time with his nephew, so she was definitely going to miss his face for the next few months. The memories of his emotional goodbye with her son Max was still fresh in her mind but remembering how Dan had sat cuddling him for nearly an hour afterwards still made her heart smile.

"Drink your coffee." She could see him lost in his thoughts, staring out of the window and wanted to keep his head where it needed to be.

"Yeah. Sorry."

"You okay?" She asked, as Dan cradled his coffee in his hands.

"Not really. I feel like I'm making a big mistake."

"That's just the nerves talking. You'll be fine when you're on the plane."

"It's not that, Issy."

She stayed quiet, letting him talk when he was ready.

"Something happened last night," his eyes were cast down now, avoiding looking out of the window.

"At the party?"

"Yeah."

"What's Chris done now?" She felt a sudden rush of Deja Vu given that Laura's boyfriend never quite understood social boundaries.

"No, for once it's not a Chris problem, although the guy is involved I guess. It's a Laura problem. Last night she told me she's in love with me."

"Ah."

"I should have known you knew."

"Yeah. She came to see me at the weekend when she'd figured it out. She needed a friend to talk to."

Dan sighed. His head was a mess and he wished he could see Laura one more time before he left.

"What did you say to her?" She asked.

"That I'd think about it and we could see about things when I got back."

"Oh, Dan for fuck sake!"

"Yeah."

"Why didn't you tell her how you feel?"

"Issy…"

"Jesus Dan! You love that girl as much as she loves you! Why didn't you just tell her?"

"Because I was scared. I am scared. I'm crazy about her Issy, but last night was very out of the blue and I didn't engage my brain quickly enough. It wasn't until I got home that I realised I should have told her."

"I've always known you were in love with her."

"I know. I've felt it for a while, although I've tried to keep it all in check. She was happy with Chris, or so I thought and I didn't want to steal that from her. I've only ever wanted her to be happy and if that's not with me, then that's fine. I'm always going to be her biggest supporter. But I know now, that I'm crazy about her and that I think I've been in love with her for a while."

They drove in silence for a time. Dan lost in thoughts of Laura and everything that he was leaving behind; Issy trying to figure out how she could rescue the situation.

As they neared the airport, he spoke again.

"Issy, I need you to do me a favour please?"

"Anything little brother. What is it?"

"I wrote Laura a note last night explaining how I feel and stuff. If she ends things with Chris, will you give it to her, please? So she knows?" He pulled out an envelope from inside his jacket pocket and held it in his hand.

"Of course. But Dan? What if she changes her mind and doesn't leave him? Do you still want me to give it to her?"

"No. If she stays with him, just bin it or something. I'll take how I feel to the grave."

"She's not going to stay Dan. It's you who she wants to be with."

"I hope that's true, I do. But we both know fear is a powerful thing. And while she might not be afraid of Chris, the idea of being alone and waiting a year for something still so uncertain may scare her so much that she can't go through with it."

He placed the letter in the centre console, between the two now empty takeaway coffee cups.

"As soon as I hear anything, I'll drop it over to her. I promise."

"Thanks, Issy."

"She'll do it, you'll see. Have you messaged her this morning?"

"No I haven't. I suspect she went home last night after the party and did it then, so I'm not sure she'll be up and awake yet. I'll let her come to me when she's ready. If I've not heard anything by the time I land, I'll message her then."

She pulled her car into one of the drop-off bays outside the terminal and turned off the engine. Dan was still looking at his hands.

"I don't want to be without her, Issy."

Dan's sister reached across the seats and took hold of her brother's shaking hands.

"You won't be. You'll see."

A few minutes later outside the terminal, Dan's suitcase at his side and his carry-on bag slung easily on his shoulder, they stood facing each other. The emotions of seeing her brother leave had gotten to her and she'd started to cry as they hugged each other goodbye.

"Look after Maxxy for me, yeah? He can call me whenever he wants and I'll make sure I bring him a new NFL jersey back."

"He's gonna miss you. We all will."

"I'm gonna miss you too."

He put his hand in his pocket and pulled out his house keys.

"Hang on to these for me? I'll just lose them if I take them with me."

Issy took them from him and pocketed them, smiling at him.

"House party at yours then."

"Go for it."

They laughed together before Dan pulled her into a final hug and kissed her cheek.

"I love you, Issy."

"I love you too Dan."

She leaned back against her car and watched him turn to walk into the airport. As he strode across the pedestrian area towards the sliding door that would take into the check-in desks, she could hear him singing to himself.

"Cause I'm leavin' on a jet plane
   Don't know when I'll be back again
   Oh, babe, I hate to go"

He's such an idiot. Issy smiled at her brother as he walked away and hoped that she'd be seeing him again, real soon.

Chapter 22

The Surprise

Midsummer: Ten Years Ago

Dan rang the bell to the Grays' awkwardly with his free hand and stepped back to wait. Within a few seconds, the large blurry figure of his godfather hobbled down the hall, mumbling under his breath about *bloody callers on a Sunday.* Opening the large white door to find his godson on the doorstep wasn't what he was expecting.

"Blimey Dan! What are you doing here? I thought you were...What. The Fuck. Is. That!?"

Dan just winked as Dave quickly stepped out of the door, pulling it closed behind him.

"That better not be what I think it is! While you might think that's a wonderful idea, it's a nasty thing to do to the man who's been your second father for your whole life."

"It's all good Dave. Don't worry. I have a plan."

Five minutes later, Dave and Dan were walking down the hallway smiling. Well, Dan was smiling; his godfather, while looking more relaxed than a few moments ago, wore a sceptical look on his face which was topped off with a furrowed brow.

"No! No no no no no!"

"Emily, relax. Genius here has a plan." Dave tried to reassure his wife as quickly as possible but secretly, he wasn't convinced that Dan had thought through his plan very well.

Emily Gray held no faith in either of the men standing before her in the kitchen, especially given what she was looking at. "Dan, she's going to university. You can't do this. For the love of…"

"Emily. Trust me. I got this." Dan winked at his godmother.

"You better Dan. Or I swear to God, I'll send Dave after you personally!"

He smiled at them both with a look that was equal parts *Look how awesome I am* and also *but you can't be mad at me can you?* However, his insides were squirming with nervousness and his arm was starting to ache.

"Right." Emily was resigning herself to this quite frankly stupid plan. "I'll go get her then, shall I?" And stalked off. Dave raised his eyebrows at Dan as if to say, *you've done it now* and taking his mug of tea, headed for the front room, leaving his godson to ponder his plan.

Alone in the kitchen, he took a deep breath and adjusted the surprise held in his right arm. He knew he was onto a good thing. There was no way this could go wrong really, but he was still nervous about it.

"Hey, you. Mum says you've got…awwwwww oh my god! Dan!!!"

Dan's heart swelled with a mixture of emotions that were

hard to put into words. Seeing Laura happy was something he loved and always had done; from the times when she was a toddler and he'd make her giggle and laugh playing peekaboo, to giving her special gifts on her birthdays which were the envy of her friends.

"You got a puppy?! Dan! Why didn't you tell me?"

"He's not mine."

"Huh? Well, he's beautiful." Laura gently stroked the tiny black and white Border Collie behind the ears and stopped talking directly to her friend altogether. "Yes, you are. You're beautiful. Yes, you are."

"He's not mine Laura. He's ours. Kinda."

"WHAT?!"

She felt like she'd just been given the best, most amazing surprise ever but simultaneously was totally shocked by it.

"Well, I know you've always wanted a dog and so I figured I'd get you one for getting into university and an early Christmas present and well, just because."

"Dan, that's a beautiful idea but I can't take him with me and it's not fair to leave him here with my parents, is it?" She looked genuinely a little sad at the prospect of having to give up a dog she'd only partly owned for less than a minute.

"Well, if you'd let me finish, that's why he's ours and not yours exclusively."

"Right, I love you but it's still early in the day so you're going to have to use sensible words for me please?"

He laughed. Laura had a wonderful way of making his heart happy without even trying.

"He can live with me until you move into your own place, whenever that is, and when you're home for the holidays he can stay with you if your mum and dad are okay with it."

"Wait? You didn't ask them!"

"Ah well, kind of. I told them I had a plan and explained parts of it."

"Dan!"

He smiled at her and gently took hold of the puppy's paws with his free hand, holding them up so the fluffy little ball of fuzz looked even cuter. "But look how adorable he is. How can you say no to those floppy ears?"

She was bursting with happiness in front of him as he carefully passed over the puppy into her arms.

"Can we keep him? Please?" She asked.

"We can. He's already got a bed and stuff at my house. I thought we could go out today and buy him some bits for when he is here with you; unless you have other plans? When you can't be with him, he can be with me."

"What's he called?" She searched his neck for a collar and tag.

"Well," Dan fished a tag out of his pocket and held it up for her to see.

She read the name etched into the metal disc. "Buddy?"

"From your favourite film."

"Dan, that's perfect." Laura nodded enthusiastically as she stared down into the dark eyes of the dog she was rapidly falling in love with. "Hey, Buddy."

While it had taken a little bit of convincing on their part, Dan and Laura had managed to bring her parents around to the idea of them sharing a dog. After a few playful threats on Dan's physical health should this all go wrong, Dave and Emily Gray couldn't help but smile at how deeply in love their daughter had fallen with the puppy she'd just met.

169

*

As Laura turned the key in the front door, she felt a sense of dread about what she was about to walk into. She knew that whatever it was, she was going to get to leave with Buddy and take him home; she'd just have to take whatever else came her way.

Chris had, not so politely, called her that morning to say she needed to come and get Buddy because he was causing havoc without her and he'd had enough. It had only been forty-eight hours since she'd walked out on him.

"He's your dog, Laura! Come get him or I'll put him up for adoption by the end of the day."

Now she was expecting a big fight while trying to get her dog back.

Closing the door behind her, Laura tensed at the silence echoing in the house where she had once lived. She shuddered and noted how it didn't feel like home any more, if in fact it ever had. Quickly from the living room, Buddy bounded out and ran straight to her.

"Hey boy!"

She dropped to her knees and hugged him, scratching him under the chin and behind the ears, his favourite.

"You're coming home with me, Buddy. We're going back to Mum and Dad's for a bit. Just you and me."

Buddy let out a loud, and excited, if not triumphant *Woof!*

Rising to her feet as the excited Border Collie spun around in circles at her feet, Laura noticed a note on the sideboard in the hallway.

Gone to the Gym. I've put his stuff in a bag. Chris.

"Arsehole!" She couldn't help saying it aloud. He knew she hated it when he left Buddy home alone unexpectedly. She would have come earlier if she knew Buddy was on his own. She knew Chris was hurting and this was just a petty attempt to get back at her but it was a shit one.

He'd never liked the idea of Buddy or the quirky relationship the dog had with Laura and Dan. The day after they'd moved into their house together, she remembered how he'd seemed less than impressed when she'd headed off to go and pick him up. At the time, she didn't really care about how he felt, she was just worried about how Dan would feel having to give up Buddy after three years of being his primary caregiver.

*

"All his bits are in the bag, there's some kibble in there too which he's nearly finished so you might as well have that, it'll just go stale if it stays here."

"Thanks, Dan. Are you gonna be okay?"

"Yeah, I'll be fine, honestly. We always knew this day was coming and it's not like I'm never going to see him again. I just thought I'd get the dog in the divorce that's all." He winked at her and flashed a weak smile in an effort to reassure her it would all be alright.

"That's not even a little bit funny." Laura smiled at him and pulled her friend into a hug. "Thank you. For everything."

Dan buried his face in Laura's neck. He was teetering on the edge of tears seeing Buddy's tail wag as he watched the two friends embrace. They stayed holding each other for a few

171

moments until Dan broke away; a worrying image flashing in his mind.

"It's fine. I'll always be here for both of you. No matter what. If he needs me, I'll be here."

"Is that just for Buddy?" She cheekily raised an eyebrow at Dan.

"Hey, I was saying the dog could come round for belly rubs anytime he wants, but I guess if you turn up for the same, I can't really say no, can I?"

"You might."

"I won't."

"I'll guess we'll see then."

*

Now as she collected the last of the dog's things, including his favourite dino chew toy which Chris hadn't put in the bag probably in a dick move just to wind her up, she realised how she felt happy to be taking Buddy away with her. In contrast to the heartache she'd felt leaving Dan's house with Buddy for the final time a few years before, this felt like it was the right thing to do and the future was ahead of her.

Buddy sat waiting at the door, ready and eager to go. Dogs just know, don't they?

"Shall we then?" Laura said as she opened the door making to leave.

He bounded down the path to her car, appreciating the fresh air and the opportunity to start anew with his favourite human.

Chapter 23

The Note

Pulling up a few doors down the street, she turned off the ignition and collected the envelope from where it rested in the centre console. She'd been to this house often and knew that the comings and goings would be minimal at best at this time of the day. Closing the car door quietly, and with her trainers making soft noises on the path, she made her way to the house, smiling at the memories of the happy times she'd spent there during the early years of her life.

For a moment she paused. The magnitude of the task she'd been given was palpable, even though the actions to complete it were easy. This was something that needed to happen. The resulting effect of what she was about to do was something everyone believed was inevitable. Very few people have a hand in the fate of others but as she quietly slipped the white envelope through the letterbox, she knew she'd just done something special.

Hearing it land gently on the mat on the other side of the door she turned and headed back to her car, knowing it was now back in the hands of the universe.

*

"Buddy, move!"

She gently pushed the curious Border Collie out of the way and picked up the envelope from the doormat. Buddy had spent the first few days at her parents' house questioning everything as he settled into his new environment. For her part, she was still finding her feet having only been here for just over a week. Her parents had been so supportive when Chris had announced that he couldn't cope with a traumatised Buddy and that if she didn't come and get him, he'd put him up for adoption.

*

"Twat!"

Laura's dad hadn't been pleased with her ex and had instantly told her to go and bring Buddy back to their house. It would take some getting used to but they'd make it work, he'd said.

"Thanks, Dad. It won't be for long. I promise. Getting on my own two feet is going to be important."

"Honey, you can stay as long as you need, you know that," her mother had told her.

*

Now Buddy sniffed her hand as she turned over the white envelope and read the front.

Laura x

That's odd. She thought she recognised the handwriting but it seemed shaky and she couldn't quite work out who it belonged to.

Sliding the flap on the back open, she pulled out a handwritten note, unfolded it and moved back to the sofa in the living room as she read.

To My Laura,

I'm not sure when you'll be reading this.

When I finish writing, I'm going to leave it with Issy and ask her to give it to you if and when you do what I think you're about to do. I guess if you are reading this, that means you've ended things with Chris and for my part in that I'm sorry. I only ever wanted you to be happy, so knowing that you're going through a breakup and that I won't be there to help support you isn't what I want. Right now, I'm sitting at home and I can't sleep. I've got a few hours before I need to leave for my flight but I can't stop thinking about last night. What you did, while maybe not done at the best time, was really brave and I'm proud of you for having the strength to do it. I've spent the whole night thinking over what I said and I feel as though I came off like a bit of a dick. Everything I wanted to say, I couldn't find the words for and now I regret not saying more. I'm not sure when you're reading this, if it is a few days later or months later but I hope it's not too late whenever it is. I told you I needed to think about what you told me and that I needed some time. I know now that was a lie that I told myself and you. I've liked you for a while Laura but it's really scary thinking about there being an us, especially with me being away for the next year. When I said last night that I didn't want to be a rebound I meant it. I hope that as you're reading this you can accept that anything happening between us straight away isn't a good idea. But even though it's not a good idea doesn't mean I'm not crazy about you. I wish I wasn't going away in the morning but we both know I need to do this. But I promise you when I'm back we will work on us if you haven't changed your mind. I have no plans to date or anything while I'm away. I'm sure of that now. I just want to focus on us and see what happens. But we need time to figure this out properly because the last thing I want is you getting hurt and me being the cause. My hope is that you're reading this letter in a few days' time because I think the waiting and not knowing will kill me. But if you are and if I'm right, I really want to spend the time we now have building something with you in any way I can. Thank god for video calls hey?! I miss you already and I haven't even left yet. But Laura, if you do change your mind about what you want, that's ok too. Just tell me and we can keep on just being friends. You know I've always loved you in my own way and only ever wanted you to be happy. But I hope that we can be more though in time.

Give Buddy a belly rub for me.

Dan x

*

Laura's hands shook as she read Dan's letter for the third time, tears running down her face. She'd put her heart on the line over a week ago. sat in the patio area of the Wheatsheaf and even though he hadn't shut her down, he had cautioned her to take her time. Now as she looked at the way he flourished his letters in his handwritten note, she felt like everything had been worth it. All she had to do was get through this year and they might be together. Her dream could come true. She just had to make it a year. She could do that, she knew it. *He's worth the wait.* Picking up her phone she messaged him, even though she knew it was some obscene time of the night for him; he would see it when he woke up.

Laura: Thank you. X

To her surprise, he replied right away.

Dan: What did I do? You okay? We good? X

Laura: Your letter. I've just read it x

Dan: Oh x

Laura: You tell me you're crazy about me and all I get is oh? ;) x

Dan: Well, you've just said thank you. You might not have liked my letter. x

Laura: Well, it had some grammatical errors and your sentence structure needs some work but it's not something we can't fix in time. Oh and I'm not sure about the possession of Laura at the start. It's a solid C+ effort. X

Dan: Ah well I guess that's my own fault for having the hots for someone good with words. x

Laura: Hots for? Oh Dan you'll tie yourself up in knots if you're not careful. x

Dan: I kinda think I already am. But poor grammar aside, I meant every word x

Laura: So what happens now? x

Dan: I think we just let things evolve without the blinkers on and see what happens. It's not like we can be together in person for a bit and I don't want this to just become a fling while I'm away. I want this to stick, you know? So let's go slow and see what happens. x

Laura: I like that. But you say let's go slow like I'm going to jump your bones? x

Dan: Chance would be a fine thing. x

Laura: Cheeky git! x

Dan: ;) x

Laura: I might tell you I love you a bit more though as the 'blinkers are coming off.' x

Dan: I'd tell you it was a bad thing but that would be a lie. Give me time and I might say it back in the same way. x

Laura: Oh Dan, you know how to treat a girl ;) x

Dan: You okay? We good? x

Laura sighed a contented sigh and thought about her answer. She was better than okay. She was fucking awesome and they were more than good.

Laura: I'm good and we're even better x

Dan: Good, so can I go back to sleep now? ;) x

Laura: You can. See you in your dreams x

Dan: xxx

Chapter 24

The House

It had been a hell of a day.

An excitable Buddy had knocked over Dave's morning cup of tea and it had gone everywhere, soaking his newspaper.

At work, she'd had to deal with a client who knew what they wanted while also simultaneously having no clue what they were doing, resulting in Laura having to hand-hold them through simple tasks that she really didn't have the time for.

Traffic coming home had been a nightmare as the road-works on the ring road where the new houses were being built were causing havoc. The resulting delay meant she was back late to walk Buddy, who, when he saw her walk through the door went nuts and nearly knocked over Emily, who was bringing Dave a drink. While his wife was fine, Laura's dad lost his second cup of tea of the day to a dog-related incident.

"Buddy!"

"Don't shout at him, Dad, he's just struggling because this is all different!"

"Well, it's different for all of us, Laura!"

Their tempers were becoming more easily frayed as each day passed while she stayed at her parents' house. While it had always been their family home, it really wasn't made for three adults and a boisterous dog and they all knew it.

"I'll take him for a walk and that'll calm him down."

Laura's mother smiled sympathetically. "It's fine honey. It'll be okay. These things have a way of working themselves out."

While Buddy stretched his legs in the park across the road, she scrolled through a property app on her phone hoping to find something she could rent and quickly but there was nowhere that would take a dog that she could afford.

Well, that wasn't strictly true. There was one place that would accept a dog and it was cheap but on closer inspection, Laura realised that it was in a really shady part of town. *Neither Dan nor Dad are going to be okay with that.*

Despondently, she walked back to the house.

She checked the time. It was just after 7 pm which meant for Dan it would be 2 pm and so he would still be working. She sighed. She really wanted to talk to him about it. He always had a way of working through problems methodically which she guessed came with age and maturity but was still something she found really hard. He'd be at work for at least another three hours so instead, she messaged him.

Laura: Hey. Had a crap day and Buddy is driving my dad nuts. Can't wait to talk later. Miss your face. X

Mercifully, a race around the park seemed to take the edge off his doggy exuberance and he settled in his bed for a while, chewing on his favourite dinosaur toy. Laura was relieved that she had one less problem to deal with for a bit.

"Sorry, Dad. I know he's gotten a handful."

"It's fine, Muffin. It's just something we have to get used to dealing with. How's the flat hunting going?"

Laura knew he was concerned and probably just trying to be encouraging, though she couldn't help but feel like he was asking less out of interest and more as a way of nudging her into moving out.

"Not great."

"Don't worry, something will come up."

By 11 pm Laura was in bed, tired from the stresses of the day, with Buddy laying at her feet. In another life, she would have happily been asleep by now but these days 11pm was the last opportunity in her day to talk to Dan once he'd got in from work.

She patiently waited for him to call like he always did.

Dan: You free? X

Laura: No I'm in bed with one of my lovers, can you give us 5 minutes and then I'll be all yours ;) x

An incoming video call made her smile and accepting it, Dan's face appeared on her phone. He was in a black t-shirt, her favourite colour on him, and was resting back on his bed, propped up by pillows, holding his phone away from his face.

"You know one day you're going to say that and mean it and

I'll be heartbroken," he said, grinning at her.

"There's only one man I'd let in my bed. You should know that by now."

"Buddy?"

"Mhmm." Laura giggled and the pressures of the day seemed to vanish. She missed his presence so much.

"Is he okay?"

"Yeah, he's calmed down, thankfully."

"I'm sorry you've had such a crap day."

"It's okay Dan. It's not your fault. Just part of being an adult, isn't it?"

"I know but still, doesn't make it any easier. Why don't you take Buddy to see Max at the weekend? They'll like that and it'll give them both a chance to blow off some steam."

"Yeah, that's not a bad idea actually. I haven't seen Issy for a week or two because work has been too busy."

"There you go then. That should pacify your parents for a bit."

"I really need to find my own place. We can't stay here. But everything I find is either too expensive or they don't accept pets."

"It's the same here. I'm not allowed pets in my apartment."

"Well, it sucks. I need to find somewhere better for him before Dad makes him live in the shed!"

"Your dad wouldn't do that and you know it!"

"No I know but I can tell his patience is being tested and that's not fair on him."

Dave had tried to be as patient as he could but a grown-up daughter and her bouncy dog in the home weren't exactly what he found relaxing, not when it had just been him and

Emily, living a peaceful existence for quite a few years now.

"My place back home allows pets."

"That's the sort of thing I need. Who was your agent?"

"Morgan Butler."

"Yeah I looked at their website yesterday, they've got nothing in my price range."

It felt hopeless but seeing Dan's face made it at least seem bearable. As he looked back at her and her beautiful blue eyes, he had a thought.

"My place back home allows pets."

"Yeah, you said."

He smiled at her. He loved her to bits but she had this uncanny way of missing the point sometimes which he found endearing.

"What?" She looked at him, confused.

Dan just smiled back, tilting his head to the side and waiting for the penny to drop.

"What Dan?" Laura knew he was getting at something but she was too mentally drained to understand it. She needed her own hand holding.

"Why don't you go stay at my place? It's sitting empty right now. It's not far from your work or your parents. And most importantly, you're allowed to have Buddy there." As he spoke, she realised it was the most sensible thing he'd ever said but she was reluctant to jump at the chance.

"Dan, it's a lovely offer but I don't know."

"What don't you know? It's a nice place, even though I do say so myself." *It was a bloody lovely place, she knew it.* "It's not like you haven't been there before, so you know it well. Obviously I have no issue with Buddy being back. You'd have your own space and I'd have someone in there while I'm away. It's a multiple-win."

"I guess I could crash on your sofa for a bit?"

"Right. Did we all of a sudden stop being us? Even if we were still only friends and weren't aiming for more, I'd still be telling you to take my room while I'm away. You'll sleep in my bed and be grateful for it." He winked and her pulse quickened.

"Dan, are you sure? I mean I know it doesn't seem like much but it's a really big deal. I'd essentially be moving in."

"I wouldn't suggest it if I wasn't sure, Laura. I want you there. If I was home and you were going through all this, I would have asked you to stay with me anyway, so why not move in while I'm not there?"

Laura had always loved Dan's place. A cute little 2-bed house on a nice quiet street, close to town. He'd put time and effort into making it really homely. She had visited often and spent time there over the years so it felt familiar and she'd always been jealous of his huge bed.

He could see she wanted to say yes.

"Laura, will you move in with me, while I'm not there?"

She laughed. It was the stupidest way of asking someone to move in with them and the dumb grin on his face told her he was genuine in his question.

She brought her thumb up to her mouth and chewed gently on her knuckle. It was a tell Dan had seen her make many times over their lives together and knew it was a sign that she wanted something, but was being shy and coy about asking.

"Is that a yes?"

She smiled and nodded, looking at him.

Dan smiled back and felt his heart flutter.

"Issy has a key. I'll message her in the morning and let her know what's going on and you can move yourself and your stuff in when you're ready. If you ask my dad, he might be able to help you on Saturday."

"Thank you, Dan. I really don't know what I'd do without you."

"You don't have to thank me, kid. Looking out for you is what I do. I'm not about to stop now."

"And you're sure about Buddy?"

"Sure as sure can be. There's obviously still space in the kitchen by the radiator for his bed and while the garden isn't huge, it'll at least give him somewhere to go when the weather is nice. I'm sure Laura. My door has always been open to Buddy. Now my home is yours too and I couldn't be happier."

"And you don't want me to sleep on the sofa?"

"I mean you can, sure. But when I come back, it might make cuddling at night a bit awkward."

"Easy there, stud! Who says you're getting cuddles in bed at night?"

Laura's belly flipped at the idea of being tangled up with Dan in his bed.

"Oh sure, because the thought of cuddling in bed is such a horrible one, right?"

"I didn't say that!" She couldn't help but grin.

"Well then. Just keep your hands to yourself and we'll be fine."

"Whoa! I didn't agree to that!"

"You won't?"

"I might."

"We'll see."

They laughed. He always had a way of fixing things and making them better and he made it seem effortless. She loved him for that. While they lay on their respective beds, thousands of miles apart, Laura couldn't help but long for a time when they could do it for real and be together in the same bed, talking and laughing together. She pictured him spooning her on Sunday mornings.

"And if you're wondering," he said grinning watching her lost in thought, "my side of the bed is on the left. You can starfish all you like till I'm back but after that, your side is the right."

"That's fine with me, I'll just have to lay on you."

"Fine by me."

"Fine."

More smiles.

"Dan, if there's stuff you don't want me to touch or see, of course, that's okay. I don't want to intrude while I'm there."

"There's nothing. You've known me your whole life. We don't have any secrets, you know that, so relax. It'll be as much your home as mine soon enough."

"Thanks, Dan. I love you."

"I know. I love you too."

She knew he wasn't saying it in the same way yet but hearing the words still made her melt even if they were only coming through the little speaker on her phone.

Looking concerned at her stifling a yawn, even though he could have stared at her all night laid back on her pillows in a white vest top with tantalisingly flimsy straps, he knew she needed to sleep and he had to let her go. As she always did, she protested and pouted at him, but eventually he managed to convince her it was the sensible thing to do.

When they'd said twenty goodbyes, she eventually left the call to sleep and Dan felt empty for a moment. Seeing her always made his day but he missed her from the very second her face was gone from his screen.

He opened up his messages app and sent a text to his sister.

Dan: Hey, Issy. How's things? Need a favour as Laura's struggling to find a place to rent.

Issy: Hey baby bro! You want me to give her your key so she can stay at your place?

Dan: How do you always know these things???

Chapter 25

The Moving Day

"Right, give me a cuddle, you!" Brian Muir drew his goddaughter into a hug and kissed her cheek.

"Thanks, Brian. I really appreciate your help." He'd been helping her move her stuff into his son's house all afternoon from where it had been stored in her dad's garage.

"Ah it's okay, you're welcome. You got everything you need?"

"Yeah, I think so. I'll pop and get some milk and bread shortly but I don't need anything else right now."

"Right, well you know where we are, okay?"

Laura thanked him and waved the car off as he drove away up the street. Closing the front door behind her and flicking the latch, she sighed. She was home. Sort of. It felt like home but she knew it wasn't her home. It was a weird mix of familiarity and newness. And she liked it.

With Brian's help, she'd moved most of her things into Dan's house and had even managed to put some of it away already, so now she didn't have much else left to do. Seeing Buddy snuggled into his bed in the kitchen by the radiator, curiosity got the better of her and she decided to wander around her new home.

Dan's house was lovely. He wasn't a neat freak by any stretch of the imagination but he was tidy and after years of tidying up after Chris, she was relieved. *The difference between a man and a boy?* she wondered.

There were, however, peculiarities around the house she'd discovered throughout the afternoon.

For example, Dan had two cereal containers in one of the kitchen cupboards. One was full of Berry Granola, his favourite. The other? Empty. She'd put her Rice Krispies in the spare one. His and hers.

By his coffee machine on the worktop, there were two matching cups. They sat easily beside each other like they belonged together.

On the sofa, there were two thick soft blankets, folded neatly on the arms at either end. As if two people were each meant to have a blanket, so they'd not be cold. It was really odd.

On the top shelf of the bookcase in his front room were two framed pictures, one of Dan with his family. The other? Laura and her family. The frames faced each other slightly so the families appeared to be smiling at each other.

And when she'd put her toothbrush into the bathroom she saw there were two pots, one for his brush and paste. The other? Empty. She claimed the second for herself and couldn't help but feel like it was meant to be. It was such a weird feeling.

When everything was away and the house explored, she sat down on the sofa and turned on the TV. The screensaver of images began to cycle in front of her. As she watched, the first few pictures were of his family, including a very happy Dan holding his baby nephew Max in his arms, but the fourth was one of her; a selfie she'd sent him the year before. She was smiling back at herself from the screen, mid-walk with Buddy somewhere she couldn't quite remember. The sixth image? Another selfie she had sent. And another and another. Laura realised that almost a third of the photos on Dan's TV carousel were of her.

If she'd been in a movie she'd have freaked out and on the verge of calling the police. But real life isn't like the movies and the thought of Dan sometimes sitting exactly where she was sat right at that moment, switching on his TV and seeing her face didn't scare her. It comforted her.

Maybe he does feel something for me already?

Her phone chirped in her pocket.

Dan: How did it go? You okay? We good?

Laura: Dan it's perfect thank you. I'm good, we're good. Your dad was a star.

Dan: I'm glad. Buddy settle okay?

Laura: Surprisingly well yeah.

She'd worried how Buddy would be when they moved again, his third home in as many weeks but given that he'd lived there for the early parts of his life; he'd settled really quickly and made himself at home. Dogs just know, don't they?

Dan: Good. Look, I need to go into the office to get a bit of work done while it's quiet. We calling later?

Laura: Yeah of course. Usual time?

Dan: Wouldn't change it for the world.

Laura: Love you x

Dan: I know. Love you too xx

*

By 10:30 pm, with fresh bread and milk in the kitchen ready for the morning, Laura was happy and content in Dan's bed, ready and waiting for his call. She was smiling to herself, looking forward to seeing him.

Dan: You free? X

Laura: Already in bed. Joining me? x

*

Dan hit the video button on the call and watched her picture come to life. What he saw was not what he expected to see. At all.

The vision of Laura in his bed was something he'd been trying to picture all day but until he saw her there, smirking like a cat who got the cream, he'd not managed to fully form the possible image in his head.

She had taken her hair down and was reclining back on his headboard in a white cotton robe and she looked incredible. It was tied up in a fashion but the top half seemed to cease to be held together around her navel and while everything that should have been covered for the sake of propriety was actually covered, it didn't leave a lot to the imagination. There was a lot of skin on show; Dan didn't know where to look.

"Welcome home." She smiled seductively with desire in her eyes.

"Making yourself at home I see?"

"Maybe. Is that okay? I thought you might like me in your bed like this."

"I mean, technically it's *our* bed now, isn't it? You seem to have claimed it. And yeah. I do like it. A lot."

She bit her lip.

"Laura, don't."

"What?"

"Don't do that?"

"Don't do what, Dan?"

"Don't bite your lip when you're looking like that. That's not fair."

"Dan, I don't know what you mean."

Of course, you don't, he thought. He wanted to be in that bed, ripping the robe from her body and devouring her in a way that just the mere thought of was making him blush.

"Boy, it's warm this evening." She wafted the collar of the robe slowly which only served to reveal more of her soft skin, so far hidden by the teasing material. He saw glimpses of curves he'd never seen before.

"Jesus, Laura. You're killing me here."

"Oops."

She had apparently found some buttons to press and she made mental notes to use them against him in the future, as they talked. Well, Laura talked. Dan just struggled to focus and comprehend the words coming from her mouth as she told him about her day and the move.

When they ended the call fifteen minutes later, Dan couldn't remember most of what was said, only how sexy she'd looked in his bed. He was torn every which way, divided by his desire for her and his reticence against taking things too far, too fast. He decided he needed a shower to cool off and clear his head.

As he walked to the bathroom he sent her one last message.

Dan: Can't believe you're sleeping in my bed looking like that.

Laura: Well firstly it's our bed you said? And secondly, I'm not sleeping looking like 'that'. It's too warm. x

A part of him was disappointed, as she'd looked incredible but as he was about to put his phone down near the sink ahead of turning on the shower, a new message from Laura pinged his device. Curiously, he opened the notification to see it was a picture message. And she was right she wasn't sleeping in her robe.

The image was something out of a dream. She was lying in his bed on her front with the covers only partially covering her body. With the phone above her head, she'd taken a picture that showed the entire length of her body, from the top of her shoulder all the way down to her calf. His eyes seemed to follow the line and curves of her figure through the picture. The front of her body was tangled in the covers of his bed but the rest of her side and bottom were exposed, clad only in a black thong which he hoped she'd chosen especially for him, knowing full well that black was his favourite colour.

Laura: Goodnight Dan. I love you. X

There was so much he wanted to say and do in reply to her message; he felt dizzy. But he did the sensible thing instead.

Dan: I know. Goodnight beautiful. Love you too x

Chapter 26

The Car

Brian eased his Ford Mondeo out into the third lane of the northbound motorway carriage and cruised past the National Express coach in lane two. It had been a good day in the city with old colleagues catching up; his first time with them since retiring. The radio was playing good songs and he was looking forward to getting back in time for dinner with Molly.

Driving the thirty five miles home that evening, he realised how much he was enjoying his retirement and not just because he didn't have to do this damned commute anymore; but because the time he could now spend with Molly made it all worthwhile. Having their relationship back to where it was when they first met was a beautiful part of growing older and he loved being able to be there for her all the time. It was like they were dating all over again.

The bus wobbled slightly in its lane as he drifted by. He checked his mirrors to make sure he had space behind him out of instinct more than reaction; nothing for at least a hundred yards. He was fine.

Brian didn't remember that the bus had continued to move out towards his car, straddling two lanes or when his Ford had spun 180 degrees, caused by his rear bumper being clipped by the advancing 15-tonne vehicle, or how it had come perilously close to being flipped over the central reservation and would have done, had his rear tyre not burst from the disintegrating metal and plastics, shredding through the rubber.

The screeching of brakes and wheels hadn't registered as he'd fought desperately for control of the vehicle, nothing really had. The airbags deploying had been loud and sudden but he couldn't remember when they'd exploded open during the whirling fifteen seconds, saving his life or why blood was now dripping down his face as he'd regained consciousness.

All he remembered, as he watched the blue lights gathering around him, through the smoke pouring out of his engine, was that the white hatchback had appeared from nowhere in front of the bus and had slammed into the side of his car crushing it backwards against the steel reinforced concrete that separated the north and southbound carriageways. Debris from the collision, including most of his car, had been scattered across all three lanes. The coach driver had mercifully been able to slam his brakes on in time so hadn't completely obliterated the rogue hatchback that had taken Brian out.

*

Fuck! Come on, Dan. Pick up!

She'd be trying to call for fifteen long, painful minutes. After each call attempt, Laura would frantically check her phone to see if there were any updates. Nothing. Aside from the fact that Molly had been informed and that firefighters were urgently trying to free her godfather, Laura knew very little about what was happening.

She tried Dan again, fear and tears causing her to shake.

"Hey you. You okay? We good?"

"Dan!" She screamed, in relief and frustration.

"Laura, what's wrong?"

"Dan, it's your dad. He's been in a crash on the motorway. It's bad. He's conscious but he's trapped. Dan, I'm so sorry."

Three thousand miles away, the bottom dropped out of his world. Like most boys, he'd always looked up to his dad in so many ways. The cliched moments that all fathers and sons have - riding bikes, playing catch, camping out - were all well and good, but some of Dan's favourite moments with his dad were more recent.

It had been his dad who'd taught Dan about finances and how to manage money which had been a critical part of the success of his freelance work, helping him to keep his head above water in the early days. Over the last few months, they'd talked at length about his trip to Canada and while Brian Muir had no knowledge or experience around the intricacies of what his son did, they'd always held counsel together when Dan needed to talk stuff through.

There was even a conversation on the morning of a New Year's Day, a few years previously, when Brian had had to pull his son aside and question his behaviour when he'd left Laura upset having shown up with a new girlfriend. In that very one-sided conversation, Dan had realised his feelings for her were more than that of simple friendship. He owed his dad a lot.

So to find out that he was now trapped in a car trying to be saved by fire crews, ripped at Dan's helpless soul.

"Dan? Are you there?"

Laura's soft voice brought him back to the present. He wanted her to hold him while he broke down, knowing that she'd keep him safe, but he knew he couldn't.

"Yeah. Sorry. I'm here."

"They say he's conscious and alert but he's pretty badly trapped so they don't know how badly he's injured."

"What happened?"

"We don't really know. Only that he got clipped by a bus and then another car hit him. Dan, I'm so sorry."

He took a deep breath and tried to calm the trembling in his hands before speaking.

"It's okay, Laura. Honestly. I should get hold of Mum and see what she needs me to do."

"No, Dan. Wait." She panicked that she was about to lose the connection to him before she had a chance to explain. "Your mum is on the phone with the police constantly. They have an officer keeping her updated who's on the scene and they're even letting her talk to your dad at points. If you call, you'll tie up the line."

"So what am I meant to do?"

"I know it's hard but she's getting updates out via your sister who's there with her."

"Fuck sake."

"I'm sorry Dan. I wish I was there for you right now. What do you need me to do?"

What did he need her to do? He needed her to be here with him so he could bury his face in her shoulder. He needed her to get his dad out of that car. He needed her in so many ways.

"It's okay, Laura. Just keep doing what you're doing."

"Are you sure?"

"Yeah. Thank you for telling me. I'm sorry I didn't see your calls."

"I just didn't know what else to do. I knew you had to know and you were my only focus." *You always are.*

"Not sure what I'd do without you."

Laura's phone buzzed in her hand with an incoming text message.

"Dan, let me put you on speakerphone. I think I have a message from Issy."

She flicked on the speaker on the call and scrolled down on her phone to find the new notification. The pause as she read drove Dan crazy even though it only lasted for a few seconds at best.

"Laura, what? What is it? Please just tell me."

"He's free. They've gotten him out."

"Thank fuck for that! Is he badly hurt?"

"I don't know. That's all Issy said. Do you want me to call her and find out more?"

"No. Stay. Please. I need you right now."

Dan wished he was home. Not just to be there for his mum. Not so he could be racing to the accident to help his dad. But also because he just wanted Laura to hold him and to feel safe. He couldn't stop shaking with the adrenaline lighting a fire in his veins.

"I'm right here Dan. I'm not going anywhere. I promise."

"Thank you."

"Are you still at work?"

"Yeah for now."

"Look, why don't you head home? I can update you when I know more. They've got him out now, it might be a while till we know more." She wasn't used to taking charge around Dan, opting usually to let him lead with age and experience, but Laura knew that he needed guidance to keep him moving forward.

"Yeah. Okay. I'll get an Uber back now. But Laura, please call me as soon as you know anything. Please."

"Dan, I promise. I love you."

"I know, I love you too."

*

The Uber took ages to arrive and by the time it did, Dan was on the verge of losing it with the helpless and unknowing driver. It was only the texts with Laura back home that were keeping him anywhere on the sensible side of calm. He knew it wasn't the driver's fault that his dad was going through hell three thousand miles away. As far as the driver was concerned, he just had another sullen passenger in the back.

Rushing out of the elevator once back at his apartment block, he had to check himself as he realised that his dad actually wouldn't be inside waiting. He was rushing for nothing. But the sanctuary of being in a familiar place while everything else seemed upside down was all he could focus on.

He called Laura as soon as his keycard unlocked the door.

"Hey, you." Just hearing her voice was like a glass of cool water on a hot day.

"Hey. I'm home. Any news?"

"Issy messaged me just as you rang. Hang on, let me read."

Dan dropped his keycard and office keys onto the table set by the side of the door and discarded his backpack on the floor by his running gear. He just needed to sit.

Rather than going down the flight of stairs to his couch he instead sat on the top step and rested his head against the bannister, hoping it would stop the world from spinning.

"So, nothing serious. Issy says he's got a few bumps and scratches but that's it. Apparently, the word miracle is being used among the firefighters. She says they're taking him to the General so they can check for anything serious but everything seems fine. He's even asking for a cup of tea already!"

"Sounds like Dad!" The relief was immense and Dan couldn't help smiling to himself.

"He's okay." He could almost hear the tears running down her cheeks as she shared his relief. "Your mum knows that you're up to date. I've told your sister."

"Laura, thank you. Honestly. I wouldn't know what I'd do without you in my life."

"Hey, we're in this together okay? You'd be doing the same

for me, wouldn't you? I love you."

"I know. I love you too."

They talked on the phone for a while, during which time Brian was being taken to the local hospital for countless scans and checks, all of which came back negative and by the following morning he was allowed to go home with a relieved Molly Muir.

It had been a very lucky escape.

Chapter 27

The Truth

"How's the head?"

"Hurts like that time we finished Grandad's bottle of whiskey at the wake."

Brian leaned back on the sofa with his iPad in his hands, looking at his son on the video call. It was nearly lunchtime for him and very early in the morning for Dan, but his son had insisted on the call as soon as he got up.

"Honestly Dan, I'm fine. Just a little bit banged up. The doctors reckon I'll have some whiplash for a bit but that's about it."

"You were bloody lucky, Dad."

"I know mate but I'm still here. I just might not drive for a bit, you know?"

Dan understood. Something like that would have terrified him too and he'd also have taken a break from being behind the wheel.

"Is there anything you need? I can ask Laura to bring stuff over if you need it."

"You'll do nothing of the sort. She's not your maid! And anyway, your mum's got me surrounded with tea and biscuits, I'll be fine."

"Dad…"

"And don't even think about coming home. I'm fine, there's no point in you flying back just to see me with a sore neck and a cut on my head."

Brian traced his fingers over the small flesh-covered plaster above his left eye.

"They stitch that?"

"No, just a bit of glue because it was deep but it didn't need anything else apparently."

"Honestly, it's a miracle, Dad."

"I know."

Dan could see his Dad was reserved in wanting to go over the events of the night before. The scary things that happen in the dark are sometimes best left in the dark.

"Dan, there's something I want to talk about with you."

"Sure Dad, what's up?"

"How're things with Laura?"

"What do you mean? I think she's okay. A little shaken by last night but apart from that, I think she's alright."

"Dan, that's not what I meant."

Brian could see the confusion on his son's digital face.

"Before the emergency services got to me last night, there were a few minutes when I was completely alone. The motorway was oddly silent, it's pretty weird in that situation to be honest.

205

But I didn't know then if I was okay or not, and for a dark moment or two, I thought that might be it. That my number had been called. Do you know what I thought about?"

"No?"

"I thought about how lucky I had been to love your mum for all these years and if this was the end, then I'd go happily."

"Dad…"

"Life is fleeting Dan and one of my biggest fears is that one day something might happen to you and you won't have the same chance."

"I don't understand Dad. What are you talking about?"

"I'm talking about Laura."

Dan sat confused watching his Dad talk, his chest tightening with each word spoken. The thing he'd resisted for so long was fighting on the surface now, more than it ever had been and the emotions of it all were starting to seep through the cracks the conflict was causing.

"I might be an old fool at times but I know what true love looks like, Dan. And I know that in your eyes she is everything you've ever wanted. You two have had a long and happy life growing up together as friends, but some people aren't destined to simply be friends. They're meant for more.

I know it's scary to admit to yourself that you're in love with her but last night should show you that life can be taken away from you in a heartbeat. Had that been you last night, I'm worried you'd have sat there regretting not telling Laura you loved her, rather than being grateful for the love you'd shared together.

We all love you and will support you whatever. Just don't

let a good thing pass you by because you're scared Dan. Life's too short to not tell the ones we love how we feel. It was the first thing I did when your mum got to the hospital last night."

He'd never been able to hide things from his dad. Even as a teenager, when he sneaked beers into his bedroom with friends, his dad had somehow known before they'd even cracked the first bottle lid. He should have known that trying to hide his feelings for Laura wouldn't have worked.

"Dad, I'm scared."

"I know. But what have I always said to you?"

"Feel the fear and do it anyway."

"Exactly. Look I'm not saying she's the one but she more than likely could be if you give the two of you a chance."

"It's hard, Dad. She's there. I'm here. We've been best friends for our whole lives and let's not forget she's basically family. It's terrifying, the idea that I could get this all wrong and the ramifications would be huge."

"Feel the fear and do it anyway."

"Yeah, I know."

"I've seen how you look at her when you're together. I've seen how she looks at you. Just tell her. Life's too short."

"I do love her. And I know she loves me."

"So what's stopping you then, you fucking idiot?"

"I don't want to tell her over the phone. It doesn't feel right."

"So tell her face to face."

"Right so, I can't come back to check on you but I can come back to tell Laura I love her?"

"No!" Brian laughed, gently so as not to aggravate his oncoming whiplash.

"What then?" This was all making Dan's head hurt.

"I think I have an idea. Do you trust me?"

"Of course! Without a doubt, I trust you Dad, although I'm currently concerned about the level of pain relief in your system and how it might be making you a bit doolally."

"Ha! Point taken but I have an idea. Let me chat with Mum and I'll message you back."

Dan hung up the call confused about what his dad had up his sleeve but he couldn't shake the feeling that all this with Laura was about to come to a head and it was about to change everything he knew to be true.

Chapter 28

The Birthday

Laura woke to her phone doing a merry dance across her nightstand. Lifting herself up on one elbow, she rubbed her eyes into focus and picked up the phone. *Dan? That's odd.* She hit *answer* on the video call and as soon as his face appeared she went back into default half-asleep mode.

"What's wrong? You okay?"

"Happy birthday!"

She heard the words but it took a moment for her brain to register them and catch up.

"Thank you," she replied, half unsure what day it actually was.

"Hey, sleepy head."

"Hey."

Dan had made an effort to wait up to wish her a happy birthday when she woke; a few more moments waiting while she figured out what day it was and what planet she was on was no hardship at all. It was cute watching her gain consciousness.

"Mhmm." Laura pulled her hair out of her face and looked bleary-eyed at him on her screen. "What time is it?"

"Seven. I know you'll be up for work soon anyway but I was too excited to wait till your alarm went off in fifteen minutes."

"Why are you awake, silly?"

"'Cos I wanted to be the first to wish you a happy birthday before your day started."

She reclined back into the pillows as her brain finally started to wake up.

"You're adorable, you know that, right?"

"Yes. I'm fully aware. I have a certificate and everything."

Laura chuckled but her heart, slowly waking up as it was, felt achy as she realised he wasn't actually in the same bed as her.

"Wish you were here though. I'd trade every present I get today just to have the day with you."

"Me too."

"Dan? Do I have to go to work? This bed is too comfortable." She wanted to spend the day wrapped up in the bed's warmth and the scent of his aftershave that clung to the sheets.

Dan laughed in a soft gentle way that felt like home. "Yes, you do. But at least you can start the day with presents."

"What? I don't think there are any here, are there? I won't be seeing Mum and Dad till later."

"Erm, well if you get your lovely ass out of bed and go downstairs, you might find some."

Laura frowned suspiciously at him. "Why do I feel like you're up to something? What did you do?"

"'Cos I am and you always know when I am. But put some bottoms or something on first."

"What? Why?" Laura protested, in part because that felt like effort and partly because she delighted in Dan knowing that she was only wearing a T-shirt and underwear in his bed while he was away.

"Trust me."

Once dressed, Laura made her way downstairs with Dan still on the video call.

"Right. I'm downstairs. Now what?"

"Go to the front door."

"Is this some sort of treasure hunt, Dan? Because I have to say it's too early for this shit if it is." The idea of being outside at 7 am didn't thrill her, but she was swooning plenty in appreciation of the special effort Dan was making for her birthday.

As she moved to the door she noticed shapes through the glass panels.

"They're not serial killers," he said reassuringly, as he spotted her looking slightly concerned at the possibility of morning company.

Opening the door she was greeted by five familiar faces. In front of her, smiling, were her parents, Dan's mum and dad, and his sister Issy.

"Happy Birthday!" They chorused.

Laura stood back aghast and nearly dropped Dan on the hallway floor.

"Let us in, Muffin. I'm gasping for a brew."

"What the...?"

Her attention was drawn back to Dan clearing his throat on the phone now held limply in her hand.

211

"I've organised you a birthday breakfast, before you have to go to work. Seeing as I can't be there, I figured this lot would be a good replacement. Max and Martin would've come too but we didn't want Max being late for school."

He always did stuff like this on her birthdays. Even from when she was little, Dan had always made a lovely fuss of her and made her big day special.

Sometimes it was glorious. Like on her sixteenth birthday, when he'd arrived in a hired sports car to take her to her party and made a scene of pulling up noisily at the venue, even opening the door for her and helping her out of the two-seater Ferrari in front of their families and a whole host of her envious friends. But sometimes more recently it had caused issues with Chris and they fought at length about his insecurities and lack of sense. She never really cared about those fights though because Dan's presence on her birthday was as important as anything in her life. But this was the first one when he wasn't actually physically present for her day. A lump formed in her throat.

"Mum! Take your son into the kitchen for me. I'll bring the birthday girl in." Issy slipped Dan from Laura's hand. "Morning little bro," she said as she passed him to her mum who continued the conversation as she made her way down the hall with the other parents.

"You okay?" Issy could see the morning was getting overwhelming.

"Yeah. It's just…I wish he was here."

"I know you do. And in his own way he is."

The girls hugged in the now quiet hallway.

"Happy birthday, Laura."

She dried her eyes with the backs of her fingers and smiled. "Thanks, Issy." She was happy. She really was. It was a lovely surprise.

Dan's sister threw an arm around Laura and steered her towards the kitchen. "Right, tea and then time for the big surprise!"

As a flurry of activity whirled around the small kitchen, Laura sat on one of the stools at the breakfast bar trying to take it all in.

Brian had taken Buddy out into the garden and was letting him spin around, chasing his tail for a few minutes. Dave was making mug after mug of steaming hot tea for everyone, while Emily and Molly were chatting away to a very tired but very happy Dan on Laura's phone, over toast and hot buttered crumpets.

"No Mum, the camera is at the top and you don't need to be that close." Laura chuckled at her mum's distinct lack of technical skills while trying to control her own jealousy for not having Dan's undivided attention.

Issy broke up the hubbub in the kitchen. "Right, someone fetch Dad in from the garden, for god's sake. Dave, sit down. Mum, give me the phone so I can put Dan where he can see."

"Thanks, sis. Feel like a sickly boy in a hospital bed right now, cheers."

"Shhh you."

Issy propped Dan up against the biscuit barrel on the kitchen side and gathered everyone around him. Then she turned her attention to Laura.

"Right. Okay. You're not a child anymore so there are no toys and crap for your birthday but we do have something special for you. It's from all of us. We hope you like it."

Laura was confused as Dan's sister passed her an envelope.

"What? What did you do?" She asked, looking at Issy who held her hands up in defence.

"Hey, don't shoot the messenger."

Looking down, Laura realised her hands were shaking.

"It's a CD!"

"Oh, Dave shut up for once!" Emily dug her elbow into his ribs. He made the same dad joke at every birthday and it was never funny but it was always hilarious to him.

Slipping the back of the envelope open, Laura struggled to comprehend what she was looking at. In front of her was a plane ticket.

"I don't understand."

"Everyone's clubbed together. You're coming to stay with me for a few days." Dan's voice trickled out of the small speaker on her iPhone 13 in front of her, causing her to focus on him. "We've sorted it with your work too, you'll fly out next week and be here with me for a few days, then fly back home in time for Christmas. I know it's not much but…"

"Shut up, it's perfect," she spoke through happy tears. "Dan, is this real? I'm really coming?"

Her smile went from ear to ear and even though looking at him, she could see he was exhausted, he was nodding and grinning.

"You're really coming."

"Happy birthday, honey." Laura's mum kissed her on the

214

cheek and hugged her and she felt her dad's hand on her shoulder.

" 'Bout time you two spent some time together again. We know how much you miss each other." Her dad squeezed her affectionately.

After lots of chatting about what it all meant, Dan spoke.

"Laura, as much as I want to spend the morning with you and this bunch of idiots, I really need some sleep. Is it okay if I go and leave you in Issy's very capable hands?"

She nodded at him and smiled. "Go sleep. Message me when you wake up." She desperately wanted to reach out and stroke the phone where his face was and tell him she loved him but she knew she couldn't. Instead, they smiled at each other as the call disconnected.

"Thanks, guys, this is amazing! I'm lost for words."

Dan's mum hugged Laura as she kept smiling through happy tears. "Go have a few days together before Christmas. I think you both need it."

With the excitement of the morning settling their parents drifted off into the living room while back in the kitchen, reality loomed.

"I need to speak to work then, and check if it's okay for me to go." Laura stood with Issy as they quickly washed the mugs of tea Dave had made earlier and cleared away the breakfast plates.

"It's sorted. I've spoken to your boss about it and everything is signed off for you."

"Oh."

"And your parents are going to have Buddy while you're

215

away."

"Really?"

"Yup. And I'll run you to the airport on Thursday for your flight. It's all sorted."

"Issy, I don't know what to say."

Turning to Laura, she placed her hands on the younger girl's shoulders and spoke. "You don't have to say anything. We love you and we can see that you're both missing being around each other. Dan has helped me sort everything. Go enjoy a few days with him and come back with a big smile on your face. Just don't tell me how you got it!"

Issy winked at her with a knowing look and then moved away.

"Right, you guys! Mush! Laura has to get ready for work and she can't do that with all of us here!"

Dan's sister always had a way of taking control of a family situation and everyone knowing the fact, would fall in line.

After a round of goodbye kisses and hugs in the hallway, Laura was left alone with Buddy standing next to her.

"Looks like I'm going on a trip, boy."

He barked and nuzzled his nose into her hand. Dogs just know, don't they?

Chapter 29

The Shower

The pavement felt hard and fast under his feet as he made his way past the stadium and turned right, back down towards his apartment; his Garmin watch beeping on his wrist to tell him he'd covered four miles.

Running to and from work was something that Dan was trying to do a few times a week while in Montreal. He'd always been a runner, so enjoyed it but he also knew it was a good way for him to work out the stresses of the day when work had felt long. He was thoroughly enjoying his time in Canada, working with a group of athletes who were getting ready for the upcoming Winter Olympics the following year but it was lonely work too and he longed to spend time with Laura. Running was a good distraction from the quiet.

It was a chilly day in the city. Winter was very much on its way but he'd gone off at a pace, wanting to have a hard run, so was soon glistening with sweat and getting warm in only a long-sleeved top and running shorts, carrying water and his phone in his black Salomon running vest. Even with the cold air biting at the exposed skin of his legs, he felt accomplished;

grateful to have a chance to burn off some energy and let his mind wander free.

Turning onto the street of his apartment block, Dan slowed to a walk, stopping his watch and saving the run, instantly transferring the data to his phone which vibrated with confirmation in the front pocket of his running vest. Taking it out to check on his run stats, he noticed a selfie sent from Laura in his messaging app. He smiled as he opened it. She'd clearly climbed into bed to relax before their regular evening video call and as ever, she looked gorgeous.

Stepping into his apartment, letting the door close behind him, he texted her as he unclipped his run vest and hung it up in its place by the door.

Dan: Hey you.

Laura: Hey you! Ready for me? X

Dan: Yeah just back from my run though, can you give me five minutes to get a shower?

His phone buzzed in his hand with the incoming video call.

"No. And I resent the implication that I should have to wait." Laura smiled, satisfied at him as he tried to feign mock exasperation.

"Apparently, I'm not getting a shower then?"

"Priorities Dan. Priorities."

She looked beautiful, curled up in the bed with a smile that he just wanted to see forever.

"You have a good day?" He asked.

"Yeah, I did. Was only a half day, because I spent the afternoon in town getting the last bits I need for my trip on Thursday."

"You're only coming for four days! How much do you need?"

"Is three suitcases too much?"

He knew she was mocking him but Dan could easily see her dragging three massive suitcases through the airport.

"No seriously, I just wanted to get some travel toiletries and stuff so I don't have to bring big bottles of things with me. Plus I wanted to pick up a book for the flight."

"Find one you like?"

"Yeah, it's called *Muse*. Looks good, some kind of love story. The reviews are great apparently."

"You'll have to let me know what it's like."

"Yeah right, okay." She knew Dan wasn't the romance novel type, but she'd let him humour her a while longer.

He walked her down into the kitchen where, after placing her on the counter against a cup, he poured a glass of water and rehydrated himself. Laura watched him drink and finding it oddly attractive, chewed the inside of her lip slightly.

"Good run?" She asked.

"Yeah, not bad, just needed to feel like I worked for it, so pushed the pace a little bit."

219

She could see the sweat shimmering on his neck, the muscles around his shoulders tense and delicious. Dan finished drinking his water, rinsed the glass, and placed it on the drainer next to the sink.

"Hot?" Laura knew he was hot but it wasn't what she meant.

"More just warm from the run. It's not hot here really. The temperatures are getting low and we're expecting snow in the next day or two which will be nice for you when you're here. Right, if you're not going to let me shower, I need to at least get out of this run top." He stripped the dark technical run top off his body, balled it up in his hand and used it to dab the sweat off his chest. Laura had seen him topless a few times in her life, even most recently on a video call when he was just going to bed but she still purred inwardly as she watched.

"You know," she said, leering unapologetically, "if I was there I could just talk to you while you showered. It's only because this is a video call that I can't."

"Huh. That's a good point." Dan smiled.

And with that, he picked her up and carried her to the shower.

"Dan, what are you doing?" Laura's brain was racing.

"Getting a shower after my run. Is that okay?"

"Erm. Yeah?"

He propped her up on the small shelf on one side of the wet room shower in his bathroom and turned on the water. Her eyes were wide in wonderment.

She watched him walk out of shot as the steam and water built up, masking her view of him. She got the impression that he was removing his run shorts but she couldn't quite be sure and it was only confirmed when he returned and stood under the falling water, that he was in fact, naked. His face and torso were all that was in view on the video call and she marvelled at how the water ran down over the muscles in his chest and stomach as her own temperature soared.

"So you all set for your flight?" He asked as he raked water through his hair with his fingers.

Laura couldn't think straight.

"Mhmm."

"Got your passport?"

"Mhmm."

"Gone a bit quiet there, kid you okay?" Dan knew what he was doing. *Payback is a bitch!*

"I'm just…yeah…mhmm," she stared like a kiddie in a sweet shop.

Back in England, Laura was aching in a way that made her unable to sit still in bed, feeling restricted by her clothes and the covers wrapped around her. The ticking inside her was getting faster by the second as she watched Dan in the shower washing himself, surrounded by steam and water spray. Just the sight of him like that was making her body react without any effort on her part.

Eventually and to her eternal disappointment, he shut the water off and wandered out of shot with a smirk on his face. Once dried and with a towel wrapped around his waist, Dan went back to collect the flustered Laura on his phone.

"Sorry about that; not enough hands to get dry and hold you at the same time."

"Oh, it's no trouble at all." She was melting three thousand miles away and wasn't sorry at all.

"Well I should probably go get dressed and make some

dinner, I'm ravenous."

God so am I. Laura's body was on fire as visions of Dan naked and wet were lodged squarely in her mind.

"Go get some sleep. And I'll message you in the morning."

"Spoilsport." She growled with a smile on her face. "I love you."

"I know. I love you too."

Dan clicked off the call smiling and went to put some clothes on, leaving Laura burning up in his bed. While she was fully aware he had known exactly what he was doing, somehow, Dan had awoken something in her body that needed to be satisfied. And it couldn't wait.

Pressing herself into his soft mattress, her back arched slightly. She closed her eyes and lost herself to visions of him, which were making her heart pound hard and fast in her chest.

A few minutes later, Laura was catching her breath; her eyes still closed but less tightly than a moment before. The heat evaporating off her body had been replaced with a comfortable longing, knowing that she'd be in his arms soon. Visiting Dan couldn't come quickly enough.

Chapter 30

The Airport

With Laura's plane touching down on the tarmac, Dan closed the flight tracker app on his phone, knowing she was safely taxiing towards him, less than a kilometre away. The relief though that she was at least on the same piece of land as him, was curdling with the anxiety of seeing her again.

Finishing the dregs of his black Americano, he pulled his arms through his down jacket and headed to the arrivals board to check on her progress.

It had been the better part of five months since they'd been face-to-face with one another. The last time he saw her in person, she'd been crying, having confessed that she was in love with him. It had taken every ounce of his emotional strength that night to walk away, knowing he had to stay on track and follow his plans for a while longer. Their paths had spent a lifetime weaving in and out of each other's lives and Laura admitting her true feelings for him had set them on course to ultimately be entwined forever. Still, it would take some time for their individual paths to become one.

For weeks they'd be talking daily, messaging and video calling each other. Gone was the pretence of just friends. She liked him. He liked her. They just hadn't talked properly about it and gotten together yet.

Each playful, flirty moment was countered with sensible grown-up conversations about their work, their individual lives and news of what was happening at home. He knew they weren't just trading flirty missives back and forth; they were beginning their journey on a serious, lifelong relationship. But without exception, every time he saw her name on his phone he'd smile and feel like a kid with a crush. He was getting foolish over her and didn't care about owning it.

Any minute now, however, she was going to walk through the security exit area of Montréal–Trudeau International Airport and shit was about to get real. Real fast.

Dan had been aching to see Laura's face again since he arrived in the country and now it was really about to happen. Digital versions of her were all well and good but actually seeing her in the flesh was a whole different level of experience and one he'd longed for since the summer, months ago.

He checked the board. She'd be here any second. He felt like one of those chauffeurs at the airport, waiting to pick up their fare, peering over the top of people in front of them, trying to catch a glimpse of who they were awaiting.

A flash of blonde shoulder-length hair drew his attention away from the group of waiting people around him but as he searched a little too frantically through the crowd, he realised it wasn't her.

His heart sank a little.

Allowing his eyes to drift away from the stranger with the

blonde hair they moved down slightly, where he spotted a pair of trainers he was certain he'd seen before. White hightops, with flashes and ticks of deep blue; the laces tied loosely, simply to keep them in place. Laura did that with her hightops.

*

Baggage claim was always something she hated, but waiting for her roller case to appear was fucking excruciating. She just wanted to go already. Didn't the Canadian ground crew know she had places to go and a very particular person to see?

Watching her pink 4-wheeled case flop on the luggage conveyor belt, Laura near enough knocked over a family of four slightly disgruntled and tired-looking fellow passengers. Normally a hugely polite and conscientious person, Laura apologised, but in her excitement cared very little. All she wanted to do was see Dan again.

Clearing customs moments later, she hurried down the corridor to the Departure hall. A set of large sliding doors separated her from the area where Dan was likely to be waiting for her and while a few yards back from the exit, the doors temporarily slid open as disembarking passengers ahead of her left into the hall.

There he was. Stood aside slightly from waiting Uber drivers and chauffeurs, a stupid big grin on his face and holding a sign that read *Laura* with a little hand-drawn love heart next to it. She wanted to cry and for a second or two, she did. But then, letting go of the handle of her suitcase and dropping her carry-on bag down to the floor, she rushed to him.

As she leapt into his arms and flung her legs around his

waist, the cute homemade sign fluttered to the floor so that he could grab her and hold on. Laura had always been a big girl and she knew jumping at him was a potential recipe for disaster but she didn't care; she was just so overjoyed to see him, that their size difference was irrelevant. Dan didn't flinch though, he just held her tight as she squealed in his ear while breathing in the notes of vanilla from her perfume. She was here. Nothing else mattered.

Not caring that she was causing a scene, Dan felt his anxiety about seeing her vanish and it was replaced by a sense of relief that she was here and everything that had been going on for weeks over text was in fact real and not some crazy wishful thinking. He felt like he was home, even though he was three thousand miles away from his actual home.

"Missed you," he said, putting her down, even though she didn't let go of him, clinging to the front of his jacket to keep him close.

"Missed you too."

"Good flight?"

"Really Dan? We're going to do the whole good flight thing now?"

That made him chuckle, referring to the basic, safe question he'd asked.

"Yup."

The coy smile he'd painted on his face however, told her she'd need to wait for more. But she could play this game for a while longer. She looked into his eyes for a few seconds more and chewed on her bottom lip; knowing full well the effect it had on him. She'd been paying attention for weeks of video calls, learning which buttons to press to get a reaction from him. It was a fun game that he seemed to enjoy too.

"Fine. Yes, my flight was ok. I slept a bit; although I'm lost as to what time it is."

Dan checked his watch, "half two in the afternoon."

"Yeah okay, I see an early night in my future."

"That can be arranged." Looking over her shoulder, Dan asked, "You reckon you should get your luggage? Or do you fancy sitting back over there in the coffee shop, so we can have front-row seats when Canadian Swat blow it up?"

She'd forgotten about her bags such was the effect seeing him had on her.

"Yeah alright, fair point." Laura smiled, reluctantly removing her grip on his jacket.

He watched her retrieve her things and appreciated how much he enjoyed watching her walk away in leggings. A part of him wondered if she already knew that though and that was why she was taking her sweet time to bend over and pick up her things.

"Eyes up front, stud," she said, pulling Dan out of his distractions.

"Sorry. Right, shall we?" He offered his arm while simultaneously taking her suitcase in his other hand.

"When did you become a gentleman?"

"Mock me all you want kid, you know full well I've always been a gentleman."

She knew he was right. He always had been the best kind of guy to her, looking after her, and making sure she was always safe. Laura melted into the idea of four days alone with Dan, just the two of them.

Chapter 31

The Day Out

The first evening at Dan's apartment was a washout. Laura's jet lag and general tiredness from weeks at work without much of a break saw her in bed before the evening got going and she slept through till well after sunrise.

Dan didn't care. He was just happy she was there. After feeding her and putting her into bed in his spare room a little after 6 pm, he'd spent the evening reading downstairs and trying to calm his nervous excitement, deciding that keeping his hands busy holding a book was probably better than waking her up to show her the sights of Montreal. That could wait till the morning.

As he climbed into his own bed that night, it took him a while to settle and wipe the stupid grin off his face that she'd given him at the airport.

*

He woke to movement near his bed, which should have scared the fuck out of him because he lived alone, but intuitively he knew who was waking him up and it didn't scare him at all. He tried to open his eyes whilst also protecting his corneas from the blinding morning light streaming through his bedroom windows.

"Morning." *God, she sounded amazing in person, first thing in the morning.*

"Hey you."

"Room for a little one?"

Dan scooched over and without thinking, lifted the cover to let her in.

It hadn't been what Laura had expected when she'd sat on the edge of his bed and watched him slowly waking up but she wasn't going to turn down this offer, so she slid in with her back to him and let him spoon her.

Both of them lay there for a moment basking in each other's warmth, awkwardly questioning internally whether this was the right thing to be doing.

"You okay, we good? Sleep okay?" He asked.

"Yeah, we're good; don't remember much after my head hit the pillow until I woke up a little while ago."

"That's good."

"You?"

"Yeah, not bad I don't think, but I could happily fall back to sleep now."

Laura bit her lip at the prospect of a lazy morning sleeping with Dan in his bed but he had other ideas.

"Coffee?"

"I thought you could happily fall back to sleep?"

Dan picked up on the coyness in her soft morning voice.

"I could but coffee is calling me, so you either get to stay here in the warm or you can come and get coffee with me."

"Wait, what? Why can't you bring me coffee in bed?"

229

"Because little lady, this is *my* bed, and you aren't drinking coffee in it."

Laura wriggled back into him, which was a dangerous move this early in the morning. Dan instinctively moved back slightly and kissed her on the shoulder, more as a distraction from his movements than a show of affection, and then quickly slid out of the far side of his bed.

As Laura rolled over to see where he had gone, she saw him pulling on a pair of grey sweatpants and near enough dissolved into his bed sheets. *Jesus wept!* She drew her eyes down from his fluffy bed hair, along the toned muscles of his back, grateful to whichever God she had to be thankful to, for the fact he slept without a top on. Her eyes carried on, sweeping over his backside wrapped in deliciously soft fabric and finally down his thighs.

Watching him stretch in front of the window was not how she thought her morning would start but *Holy Fuck* she wouldn't change it for the world.

Turning, he asked, "you still like your lattes?"

"Some things don't change, Dan." She followed him with her eyes as he moved across the bedroom.

"Right, well get your ass out of bed and I'll make you one."
How isn't he cold without a top on?!

"Mhmm, sure thing." Laura needed a minute to compose herself as suddenly she couldn't feel her legs.

Finding him downstairs in his kitchen moments later, she smiled as he handed her a latte.

"So what's the plan today?" She asked, hoping he'd suggest just staying home and ravaging her all over his apartment, she reckoned the kitchen counter would be perfectly secure.

"Well, I really want to take you to see the sights. It's a lovely city and my place is on the edge of a historical bit, so it looks pretty this time of year with all the lights and stuff. Then I thought I'd take my favourite girl out for some lunch and then afterwards," he shrugged slightly, "we'll see what we're in the mood for."

"Sounds good."

"It will be, I hope."

She smiled at him, she couldn't help herself.

He coyly smiled back, noticing the tension in the room going up a notch.

"Sugar?" He asked, nodding at her coffee.

"No thanks Dan, I'm sweet enough."

He ruefully shook his head and smirked at her. "Are we really going to do this all day?"

"Oh I think so, don't you? I mean I could stop if you'd rather?"

"I think you misunderstood my question for a complaint."

Sparks weren't going to fly at this rate, the whole bloody apartment block was going to explode.

"Right, if that's the game plan all day, I'm going to go take a cold shower and cool off while you drink that coffee, otherwise we'll never leave this place today."

Spoilsport. She watched him leave, smiling behind her coffee.

When she left England, Laura knew she was excited to see him but was really overdoing the playfulness this morning and she knew it. *Keep it cool Laura.* The last thing she wanted was for things to get awkward with him.

Standing under his wetroom shower, Dan tried to calm himself down. His body was crying out for one thing and his mind wanted another; terrified of going too fast, too soon and blowing the whole thing before it had a chance to get going.

All those video calls and messages they'd shared over the last five months, had left him feeling like she was the one and the last thing he needed to do was to fuck this up. He wanted to do this right. He knew he loved her but he didn't want her visit to all be about lust and fun; he needed her to see that he wanted her in his life.

As he rinsed the body wash from his skin, he turned to the door and wondered how he'd react if she walked in on him showering right now. Deciding not to find out, he shut the water off and grabbed a towel from the rail. *Keep it cool Dan.* Today he knew, was going to be a challenge.

*

When they eventually got out of the apartment an hour later all bundled up in layers of warm thick winter clothing, they eagerly started to explore. As it was Christmas time, the city was awash with the colours and lights of the festive season; Laura felt like she was in a low-budget Netflix movie and she loved it.

The day began with Dan giving her a tour of the historical district of Montreal and the Notre-Dame Basilica. It was breathtaking in the glistening falling snow. While he was no history expert, he took time to show and explain to her what he knew about it, which was in truth very little, but she hung on every word.

Stopping for coffee mid-morning, he took her to a sweet little Hawaiian coffee shop down by the waterfront and they sat sipping hot coffee from giant yellow mugs, getting lost in the magic of it all. They talked about Dan's coaching work in Canada and how he was grateful for the opportunity. Laura felt as though she could sit and listen to him talk for hours and she wouldn't care if they lost the day to it, she was in her happy place. This is where she belonged. Not in the country but in Dan's company. Nowhere else felt quite the same.

They walked along the waterfront and soaked up the views as they talked about how it felt for her living in his place and how Buddy was doing a lot better now he was settled. He missed that damn dog, even though he'd not really spent a lot of time with him before he left for Canada, but he knew that Buddy would take care of her for him when he wasn't there and that was reassuring.

By lunch, the snow was really starting to fall, adding to the thick, white, freezing blanket that covered the city. More than once, he thought about pulling her into him and kissing her under the Christmas lights but kept chickening out at the last minute thinking it would be too twee.

"Oh, my god. How cool is this place?"

Laura lit up as she looked around the cute little American-style burger place Dan led her into for lunch.

"It's not a big chain place, but the burgers are good and the shakes are even better."

"You had me at burgers, Dan. You put a milkshake in me and I'll not be responsible for my actions."

Not for the first time that morning, Dan struggled with

knowing how to respond. She'd been leaving him wanting to say more all day but he didn't trust his mouth to connect with his brain and anything he did say would be taken down and used against him; he was sure of that. So instead, he ordered them cheeseburgers and fries each, accompanied by two ridiculously large, creamy and gloopy chocolate milkshakes that were so thick, the straws stood upright without any kind of support.

As they ate, Dan realised that a growing part of him didn't want to be in Canada anymore really. He just wanted to be wherever Laura was; the location was irrelevant.

Laura slurped the last of her milkshake from the glass and sighed a long contented sigh.

"'S'up, buttercup?" He asked.

"I'm full of burgers and milkshakes. I'm a happy girl."

He smiled. "It's good to know that I can make you happy."

"Easy, stud. It's all the burgers and chocolate milk." She winked at him, twirling the straw with her fingers provocatively and knew full well it was entirely him that was leaving her warm and fuzzy.

"Is that right, kid?"

"Mhmm, and if you're not careful Dan, I'm gonna have to show you I'm not a kid anymore."

Dan nodded and bit his lip, thinking about all the ways she could show him that; eyes locked onto one another like heat-seeking missiles, as if they were each daring the other to blink first.

The tension went up another two notches.

Deflecting, Dan asked, "What are you in the mood for tonight?" Causing Laura to raise an eyebrow before he quickly added, "for dinner. I'll cook back at the apartment."

A laugh escaped her and they both burst into a fit of giggles, garnering the attention of the owner of the burger place, who smiled to himself at the sight of love and went back to counting the cash in the till.

Dan looked at her as she regained her composure and moved the now-empty milkshake glass off to the side. He was truly in love with her. It was shameless and he didn't care. No woman would ever be as beautiful, as funny, or as passionate as she was and he completely accepted that they'd be together forever. He wanted to love her until the day he slipped into a forever sleep, no longer able to draw breath. Laura Gray was his home. He'd fight for her and defend her against any invading host; his life was hers completely.

He resigned himself to his fate.

Outside, after they'd wrapped themselves back up in all their warm layers, the pair stood in the falling snow.

"Let's have a picture together!" Laura announced, fumbling for her phone with cold hands.

Dan caught it before it hit the ground and flicked open the camera app before handing it back. She smiled and looked longingly into his eyes like a puppy in a shop window, looking for an owner.

Holding the phone up in the standard selfie position, Laura backed herself nearer to Dan and was about to hit the shutter button, when she felt his arms around her waist, pulling her gently back into his body. She turned slightly and looked up at his face to see him smiling, looking back at her. She wanted nothing more than to lose herself in his face forever. *CLICK!*

Even though she'd taken the selfie, they held each other's gaze for a moment, fearing that they'd break the spell if they looked away.

Eventually, Laura blinked first and drew her attention to the phone and the photo she'd just taken. They looked in love; her heart raced as she felt like it could actually really be happening. He'd said in the summer they'd have to wait a year before taking things further and yet here they were, outside a burger place in downtown Montreal, as the snow fell, both caught up in yummy feelings of love.

"It's a nice one," he said, looking over her shoulder. "Send it to me?"

Laura hit share on the photo and airdropped it to Dan. A few clicks later and he spun his phone around for her to see, showing her that he'd set it as his wallpaper. Like couples do.

She bit her lip and smiled, her heart bursting under the weight of love she felt for him. Dan looked back into her eyes and returned her smile, a knowing look on his face, saying everything that was as yet unspoken between them.

"Why don't we head back to the apartment for the afternoon and see if there's a film we can snuggle up and watch together for the rest of the day? It's probably better to watch the snow fall from inside rather than out. I don't want you getting any colder."

"Have you got popcorn and a blanket too?"

Dan just smiled and took her hand as they made their way back to his temporary home.

Chapter 32

The Dinner

"How do you like it?"
"Dan, you can't ask a lady that!"

*

The afternoon at Dan's apartment had developed from chilled and relaxed, to playful and borderline flirty. And now things were heating up. Literally.

Arriving back after lunch, Dan had sorted the snacks and Laura had picked the movie. The mix of toffee-coated popcorn and a low-budget love story with actors they had never heard of, was a perfect accompaniment to the thick warm blanket thrown over them both. Within the first quarter of an hour, they'd worked out the plot and she'd slid nearer to him, snuggling under his welcoming arm. Sometimes they went for the popcorn bowl at the same time, just so they could touch hands unapologetically.

As dusk descended on the city, pretty mood lights automatically glowed into life around the apartment.

"Really? That's your move, stud?"

"You wish. They're on timers."

"Sure they are, smart guy!" But she didn't care. She felt spoilt and lucky.

Dan smiled and relaxed into holding her, encased in their blanket but his mind was still conflicted. While he knew he was in love with her, he still couldn't get past the idea that they were basically family. She was here and it was just the two of them and for all intents and purposes it should have been perfect, but niggling doubt gnawed at the edges of his consciousness.

As the movie ended, Dan rose to go top up their drinks and put the now-empty popcorn bowl on the counter. With the whole couch to herself, Laura simultaneously spun and slid down, to lay horizontally along its length smirking at him as he returned.

She expected some quip or sarcastic comment as she lay looking up at him, upside down. Instead, he simply leaned down and gently kissed her on the nose, doing so slowly and purposefully. It made her tingle all over. He hovered over her for a moment as they smiled at each other.

"Is it okay if I go get ready for bed?" She asked with a grin. "I'm not tired, I'm just done with regular clothes for the day and I'd like to be comfortable."

"Of course. Go for it. I'll start dinner."

Watching her walk up the stairs, he wondered if there was a certain spring in her step or if he'd just imagined it. Then he speculated what she'd come back down in, as opposed to *regular clothes*; his mind slipped to lace and lots of skin and her hair down. He loved it when she wore her hair down.

"Hey! What happened to starting dinner?" Laura had that smile on her face, the one she always had when she was feeling playful. She knew exactly the game she wanted to play and she was just about to make the first move.

"Erm yeah, sorry. Daydreaming." *How long have I been thinking about that??*

He pulled his focus from his thoughts and into the present, to the woman standing in front of him. *I'm dead!* If this was *irregular clothes* he was here for it and never wanted to leave. She stood a few feet away, wearing maybe just three things and clearly leaving a whole lot to the imagination that his mind struggled to process. For God knows what reason, she was dressed in his one of his old NFL jerseys that fitted her to perfection. It clung to her body in a way that would have drowned sailors at sea, had she been a siren. She was calling to his vision and he feared for his life. The length was just long enough that it covered her bottom, skimming her mid-thigh and without wanting to openly stare, he was as sure as he could be that she wore nothing underneath it.

She accompanied this feat of wonder with a pair of fluffy pink socks. Laura always hated her feet being cold so her sock collection was vast. Dan knew, however, his eyes wouldn't be focusing on her feet much if he didn't pull himself together.

"Eyes up front, stud." She revelled in the game she was

playing. Her first move had taken at least two of his pieces off the board and she was going to enjoy leaving him defenceless and exposed as she went in for the kill.

"Pretty sure I had one just like that…" he said, noting her guilty look.

"Hey if you're going to leave me alone with all your things, what am I meant to do?" She made to grab the hem "I'll take it off if you like…you can have it back?"

"NO NO, it's fine. You keep it. It's yours now."

Dan made an attempt to walk to the kitchen without arousing suspicion and hoped the head rush he got was just from standing up too quickly.

He grabbed a skillet from the counter where it lived and turned on the heat, adding a little oil and salt as he went.

She watched as he prepared a green leafy salad while he waited for the pan to reach temperature. Laura could feel her own heat rising at the same rate.

The kitchen in Dan's apartment wasn't huge, leaving them having to move carefully around each other as he cooked and she collected cutlery and opened a bottle of wine. In actuality, there was plenty of room for two people to work in the space but it didn't stop them from making excuses to brush past each other.

Laura moved across in front of him as he grabbed two delicious 10oz steaks from the fridge and they stood in a stalemate with her back to the stove.

"How do you like it?"

"Dan, you can't ask a lady that!" Her body pressing against his.

"I meant the steak." He kept his eyes on her as he placed the plate of meat beside her.

"I'll like it however you give it to me." If she'd been a cat, she'd have purred as she playfully raised her eyebrows.

"Laura Gray, you will be the death of me."

She wanted to reach up and bite his bottom lip and tell him she wasn't hungry for steak any more but instead she just mentally took a few more pieces from his side of the board and went to pour the wine.

The steaks hit the pan with an explosive sizzle, fat and oil spitting joyously into the air. Dan added more salt and seared the meat for three minutes on either side. She thought it smelt divine and her mouth watered, not for the first time that afternoon. He looked good. She couldn't deny it.

His soft white buttoned-down shirt sat gently on his body, showing the muscle definition in his chest and shoulders. Dan wasn't a ripped muscly guy but he kept himself in shape and she was grateful for it as her eyes drifted slowly down his body. A thick leather belt with a patina-speckled buckle wrapped itself like a serpent around the belt loops of his stone-washed blue jeans. In contrast to Laura and her fluffy cosy socks, Dan hated anything on his feet so stood frying steak barefoot. Lost in desire, she forgot if she'd poured the wine yet or not.

Dan dropped the cooked steaks onto each of their plates; her belly growled on multiple levels. *Damn it!* He'd just taken a piece of her own from the field of play. He'd often eaten with her over the years and made her simple snacks and meals but this trip was the first time he'd cooked properly for her since she'd realised her love and desire for him. As turn-ons go, it was a niche one, but having him cook for her was driving her crazier than any pickup line or dirty talk ever could. He was a carer, ensuring her needs were met, and she wondered how far that mentality would extend. She was ravenous but not for steak.

They ate quietly with their plates on their knees, sat on the sofa. The growing fire burning between them crackled and popped as they kept eyeing each other. Upon Laura clearing her plate, Dan presented her with an individual strawberry cheesecake as dessert; her favourite.

"Burgers and milkshakes and now steak and cheesecake? Are you trying to get on my good side, Dan?"

"Am I not already on your good side, kid?"

"Maybe you were but you just fucked it calling me kid." The wink told him he wasn't in any doghouse.

"Sorry, force of habit." His usual half smile.

"No, it's fine. You do you, stud. It's just hard to think of myself as a kid when I think the things I do about you."

As she spoke she scooped the crumbs of the biscuit base of her dessert into her finger and sucked it clean innocently. He watched her mouth.

"What's that supposed to mean?"

Taking his empty dessert plate she rose and sauntered to the kitchen, Dan following her as she placed the crockery by the sink.

"Well let's say what I think about you, my friend," Laura added with a look that said they were anything but friends "is definitely more the kind of thing a woman would think."

She spun around him dragging her fingertips across his stomach as she moved back towards the sofa. His gaze dragged his body around to follow her as she leaned back against the cushions.

"You're full of riddles tonight."

The fire wasn't crackling and popping anymore; it was roaring and about to engulf the whole place.

"Would plain simple English be better for your brain, Dan?"

A shake of the head and a roll of his eyes, told her he had very few pieces left on the board. The game was coming to a head so she went in for the kill.

"You know I'm in love with you, Dan. I've made that clear. But with that love comes, how shall we say, wants and desires."

"Oh."

"So because of those desires, that means my mind… wanders." She bit her lip and twirled the tips of her blonde hair around her fingers. Two things she'd learned on video calls over the past few weeks that drove him crazy.

"I…erm." Dan was on the back foot and fully aware he was being beaten by a more advanced game player. He was in trouble.

"I think about you when I'm alone. I think about you when I shower. I think about you when I'm naked in *our* bed."

"Laura. Stop."

"Stop what Dan?"

"You know exactly what I mean!"

"Do you think about me like that Dan?"

"What?"

"Do you…think about…me…like that?" She stared at him and waited for him to answer. She knew the game was about to be won.

Chapter 33

The Night

Standing by the couch in his two-floor apartment, Dan looked at her, trying to fight the onslaught of thoughts and emotions that risked crashing over him like a tidal wave. He knew he wanted her, he'd been conflicted about it all day in her company and he was fully aware that Laura was now pressing his buttons intentionally.

"'S'up buttercup?" She said with a devilish grin on her beautiful face, flicking her eyebrows up.

"You know exactly what's up," he replied, raising his own eyebrow at her.

"It was a genuine question Dan, I don't know why it's causing you such an issue." She leaned provocatively against the couch in his NFL jersey and her fluffy socks.

"Because it could open up a box that so far, we've avoided opening."

"So you don't want me to know?"

"Laura."

"Dannnnnnnnnnnnnnnn."

"God, you're a pain in the arse sometimes."

She winked at him. "But you love me so it's okay."

"That's not the point!"

"So do you or don't you?"

"Laura!"

"Oh come on. What's wrong with the two of us saying if we think about the other in that way or not? Is it a bad thing? You told me once before that you dreamed about me...."

"For fuck sake." He couldn't help but laugh with her. "Fine. Yes."

"Yes what Dan?"

"Yes! I think about you like that."

Laura just nodded and smiled to herself, claiming his last piece on the board. The victory was hers.

"The thing is Laura, if you hadn't told me you loved me in the summer, we wouldn't be having this conversation right now."

Confused and worried, Laura replied, "What do you mean?"

"Because with the thoughts I'm having about you, you'd be in my bed already and that jersey would be somewhere on the stairs. Game on. But you had to go and bring love into it. And now I have to try and be a gentleman..."

"That's big talk, Dan."

"You wanted to know if I think about you like that or not? Well, I do. And right now doing the right thing is very far from my mind." He took a step towards her.

"Oh."

"I think about you a lot." He took another step.

Without meaning to, for a change, she bit her lip. He was so close to her, she was sure he could hear her heart racing and see the heat haze coming off her skin.

"What's stopping you from taking it further?" She asked tentatively.

"The worry that we might fuck this up."

"We won't."

"We might."

"Okay. Are you worried that I'll think you just want a one-night stand?"

"I don't want that."

"You might."

"I don't."

"Promise?"

"I always keep my promises."

He closed the last step between them. There was a pause and they looked at each other, electricity pulsing between them.

Dan realised that it was time to let go of the notion that she was like a sister to him. She wasn't any more. She was a beautiful, classy and sexy-as-hell woman and he was crazy about her. Blood pumped in his ears and his mouth went dry. He wanted to take her to bed and lose himself with her under the covers until it was time for her to fly home in two days' time.

He could smell the vanilla on her skin. The aroma seemed to hang in the air around him, making his chest tight in the best way possible. He noticed the curve of her lips, and that they looked as soft as they'd felt ten years ago on New Year's Eve.

And that fucking shirt.

It seemed to cling to her in all the right places, drawing his eyes and his attention away from the safety of remaining only her friend. He hoped she'd not be upset if it got ripped during what he was now considering doing against his better judgement. He needed to touch her. To feel the heat on her skin. To hear her ask him to take her in every way imaginable.

"Laura…"

"Dan, shut up and kiss me."

He didn't need telling twice. Sparks flew as they kissed, his body pressed so hard against hers that it threatened to topple her over the couch so she had to fight back. Grabbing him hard and kissing him back struggling to stop herself from ripping his shirt buttons open.

It was as if the pressure valve on their attraction to each other was finally opened and it was causing them to let go of every doubt and hesitation they had.

Dan's hands were under her top, his fingertips digging into the soft flesh at her hips, pulling her into his body while his lips pushed forward, causing her to have to lean back to keep her balance.

Her fingers worked quickly at the buckle on his belt and pulled it free from the loops of his jeans before dropping it on the floor. As she did so, she took the opportunity as Dan looked down at what she was doing to push him playfully away.

"Come get me," she purred, as she turned and slunk her way up the stairs that lead to the bedroom. Slipping his jersey over her head as she took the first step, she held it to her bare chest and looked back over her shoulder. *Thought as much, nothing underneath it.* Dan was transfixed. "Somewhere on the stairs, right?" Continuing upwards, she let it slide off her fingers where it landed on the second highest step and then turned left into his bedroom.

By the time Dan caught up with her, she was lying naked and exposed on his bed looking like a Rubenesque work of art, smiling as if she belonged there, her socks left discarded on the floor.

With his shirt thrown somewhere he'd have to remember in the morning, he climbed over her and kissed her with a softer passion than that of a few moments before. Her hands pushed urgently at his jeans until they were lodged awkwardly around his knees. Dan didn't care. She was finally here. Naked in his bed. He took them off the rest of the way without his lips ever leaving hers.

Laura's fingers slid up over his shoulders and tangled themselves in his short hair as they kissed. She was really doing this. Kissing him in his bed. It was happening.

Pulling his lips from hers, he left a trail of kisses down over her chin and along her jawline. Three soft gentle kisses connected her jawline to her collarbone via the pale skin of her neck. And then from her collarbone, it took five more kisses for Dan to find the centre of her chest. Her body tingled in all the right places and she started to close her eyes.

And then he disappeared, descending her body with ease, vanishing underneath the white bed sheet he pulled up over him as he went. This wasn't something he was doing through feelings of obligation or because he just wanted to do it to make her happy, he was doing it because there was nothing else in the world that he yearned to do more, this was how he wanted to begin pleasuring her.

"Uhhh! Fuck!" Laura's back arched as though some sci-fi alien was trying to escape her very existence. Grabbing the sheets around her instinctively, hoping it would keep her grasp on the land of the living, fireworks exploded in her brain, blinding her senses and making her body quake.

There was no clumsiness in Dan's work; it was done with precision and intent as he quickly learnt and assimilated what her body responded to. He gradually built the pressure and tension lodged in the pit of her stomach, until it threatened to overwhelm her, dragging her over the edge of the cliff he held her on. She was in heaven and she never wanted to leave.

Then he did the unthinkable...he slowed.

NO! She didn't need slow, she needed urgency and she needed it now! She needed to fall off that cliff and break into a million glorious pieces on the rocks below.

"Dan please!" She begged, grabbing the top of his head, as he edged her painstakingly slowly to what she craved. "Please!"

But he knew what he was doing and smiled to himself. He knew holding her here for a moment would make it all ten times better for her. This wasn't about his pleasure but hers. She deserved this.

Involuntarily, in trying to control the convulsions of her body, Laura's hips drove down the bed, right into Dan and it didn't matter that he was holding her on the edge anymore; the cliff just disintegrated around her without either of them meaning it to. A huge orgasm crashed over her and she cried out, her body cramping as it did.

She was about to let out another expletive, but his lips found hers before she could form the words in her mouth, and he held her and kissed her as she shook; his firm, toned naked body above hers. *Jesus, he felt good.*

On regaining a mild level of consciousness, Laura grinned and pushed him onto his back. "Neat trick," she said breathlessly, biting her lip. "Now it's my turn."

For the next hour, they made love, like they'd done it for years, each of them pushing the other's buttons until one of them tapped out or until the pleasure became too much for them to bear. They only stopped when Dan complained that if he didn't get a drink, he was going to pass out.

Laying on his chest afterwards, tangled up in the sheets as they calmed down, his fingers slowly tracing small circles on her back and with post-orgasm tremors still rumbling through her body, she had never felt more at peace but she knew she couldn't hide from the large elephant sitting in the corner of the room.

"This doesn't have to change anything you know? Not if you don't want it to. It can just be sex. We can still work on us when you get home."

Laura knew it fucking changed everything, but she wasn't about to make Dan feel like he had to commit to her if he didn't want to. If this was all it was, at least they'd always have one magical, mind-blowing night.

"Laura, it changes everything. And I want it all to change. I know it's been a few months now since that night in the bar…"

"When I told you I was in love with you," she interrupted.

"Yes…that's the one," he grinned, "but like I said in my note," he pulled her closer to him, "I'm crazy about you and I have been for a while."

She buried her face in his chest and waited, too scared to move in case it woke her from the dream she felt like she was in.

"I just know a long-distance relationship is going be fucking hard. For both of us."

Dan felt like he'd just given her an empty gesture. That he'd made love to her and left her with no promises of a future together. It left him feeling awful.

"It's you I want, Laura."

She lifted her eyes to his. *God, he's got pretty eyes.* "You mean that?"

"Yeah. You have been my favourite person since you were a baby and if I'm honest, I fell in love with you a long time before you found the courage to tell me. I was just scared of admitting my feelings to myself."

"Why?"

"Because you're like family Laura but I've realised these past few months, being here, that also means I need you in my life."

"Like a sister?"

"No, not like a sister."

"Oh."

"You, Laura Gray, are everything I want my world to be wrapped around. I am lovingly and completely yours."

She lifted herself from his chest and spun slowly to sit on the edge of the bed, her back to him, the soft light of the bedroom making her bare skin glow.

"But? I sense there's a but here."

Dan sighed and moved behind her and lovingly kissed her, where her tattoo sat above her shoulder blade. "But you know I can't leave yet. I have another seven months on my contract here." Just saying the words tore his heart in two.

She pouted. She always pouted whenever she didn't get what she wanted from him; she'd done it her whole life and wasn't about to give up the habit now at twenty-eight, sitting naked on the edge of his bed. "I know."

"And you can't stay here. You know you can't."

Fuck him for always being right.

"Laura, I want us to be an us. But we have to wait to be together until I get back until we can be like a normal couple. I just don't see another way."

"Me either. Dan, I just want you. If I have to wait every day to be with you, then so be it."

"I love you, Laura. I'm in love with you. No one will ever have my heart but you."

"Do you mean that?" She asked, turning to him and looking into his bright, blue eyes.

"Mhmm." Dan stroked her face and smiled, realising he could never love anyone else again.

Rather than an affectionate touch or a loving kiss, like Dan expected her to give, Laura placed her hands on his chest and forced him onto the flat of his back, grinning as she climbed on top of him.

"Then we have about thirty-six hours to make the most of each other. I hope you're hydrated

Chapter 34

The Leaving

Dan watched her disappearing through the security doors and sighed, before heartsore, trudging back to his car. Wanting to hide from the world, he pulled his hood up over his head, so it hid his face as he walked out of the terminal, keeping his gaze down as he fought to keep his emotions at bay.

The past thirty-six hours had been a wonderfully heady mix of passion and intimacy, as they had lost themselves to their love for each other. It was as if they'd always been together in that way. Moments of heated passion had spilt over from the bedroom to the shower and then the kitchen, and a few times on the sofa. Each time had been followed by long spells of intimate talking, holding each other and cooking together.

They spent those hours in constant physical contact with one another, scared that if one of them let go, the other would float away into the ether to be lost forever. As they walked they held hands. If they were sitting together on the sofa, she would tangle herself up in him. Even as they slept, they kept their feet on each other the whole night.

There was even a video call to her parents, to update them on her flight home, where Dan had teasingly been dragging his fingers across the indentation at the base of her spine, out of sight of the camera. It was a place he had learned early on, drove her crazy when he touched it in the right way. That video call ended abruptly. And for a few heated moments, they forget about anything other than their need to connect.

He needed her and she needed him and everything else could be damned as long as they had each other.

That morning had been reserved in comparison to the hours that had gone before it. They'd laid in his bed tangled up together for a long time before either of them spoke, both wanting to savour the warmth and the feeling of the other. And lying there in the stillness, it was as if their hearts were becoming bonded forever.

Reluctantly and with a lot of protesting from Laura, they had gotten out of bed eventually and made ready to leave the apartment. He had to keep them both moving for his own sake as much as hers because he knew if they stopped, the weight of her leaving would consume them both. For her part, she was grateful that he was keeping gentle control of the situation as she knew at any moment it could all easily become too much for her.

Walking into the airport, he'd carried her bags and held her hand. Her soft fingers intertwined with his, the warmth from her palm against his own. He never wanted to let go.

As she checked herself onto her flight home, Dan waited with a smile as he watched her move. Something about her made him feel like she would always mesmerise him and he was glad of it. She was like a painting he could sit in front of and stare at all day, never tiring of its beauty.

When she returned she'd asked what was making him smile, he'd just kissed her on the nose and said it was her.

"I don't want to go," she said, pulling herself into him.

"I know. I don't want you to go either."

"This feels worse than when you left in the summer."

"This is different though."

"Well, it doesn't feel different." She buried her face in his jacket and let the tears fall gently.

"Of course it is, Laura. When I left in the summer, we didn't know what was going to happen. But now the prince has his princess and it's time for the happy ending. We just need to wait to start the celebrations until I get back in a few months."

"You're such a soppy bastard, you know that? But I love you, Dan, with all my heart."

"I love you too, Laura."

He held her close and kissed the top of her head, smelling the vanilla perfume that surrounded her. His mind flashed through moments of the last few days. Laughing and joking over burgers and milkshakes. Walking in the snow, holding hands. Kissing her passionately against her sofa. His fingers on her skin. Taking cute selfies together. Watching her smile. Feeling her naked body next to his. Kissing her neck.

"We'll be okay, baby. I promise. You'll see."

They kissed goodbye at the entrance of the security checking area and didn't care that the guard looked on disapprovingly as they did. Her tears trickled down her cheeks as she stepped back and let her fingers slide out of his grasp. It was too painful for either of them to articulate.

As he watched her blonde hair disappear from view, Dan felt properly lost for the first time in his life.

By the time he got back to his apartment, the acute loss of her leaving had been replaced by an odd numbness that he couldn't make sense of at first.

Shutting the door behind him, as the lock clicked into place, he noticed a hollow sound to the space that he hadn't previously felt. He shook his head slightly in an effort to focus and removed his coat, hanging it up on one of the hooks by the door. As he did so, he noticed the emptiness of the hook next to it which had accommodated Laura's big puffer jacket over the last few days. Her absence was profound.

Heading down to the kitchen area, he spotted the cup that she'd made her morning tea in before they'd left. Her soft pink lipstick sitting on the rim. Those lips had been on his that morning and they'd tasted like strawberry lipgloss and forever.

Leaving her cup where it was, it didn't feel right to move it yet, he turned into the living area and spotted the pillow she'd casually thrown off the sofa the night before so she could lay across him. Picking it up, he rested it against the wall. It didn't belong on the sofa now. She did.

The hole she'd left in his life threatened to tear him apart. This was no longer his home. It was the place she was not. And he didn't want to be there anymore.

The practicalness of his brain engaged and he told himself to pull it together. *It's just a fucking pillow.* He threw it carelessly back on the sofa and went back into the kitchen, where he quickly rinsed her cup, putting it away before shutting the cupboard door on it loudly. *She's going home. She's not fucking dead.*

With his insides raging, he leaned on the kitchen counter for support.

Three thousand miles away.

He fought as best he could. Screwing his eyes up and gripping tightly with his hands on the woodwork.

It's only a few months.

The ringing in his ears was deafening and his arms shook from the effort of holding himself up as he fought desperately to hold back the tide.

And then it hit him. At first, it was a strangled sob as he tried to focus and keep fighting. But one sob followed another and soon the pain of her leaving crashed over him and he cried heavily in the kitchen, resting down on his elbows so he could hide his face in his hands.

As he cried, he realised that she'd never be back here in this place with him and he resented the apartment for that. He thought about her being back home and spending time with their families over Christmas and New Year, and he was jealous of them for that. He considered that his job would keep him here for another seven months and he couldn't give a single fuck about his work anymore.

Laura was his everything. She always had been. And he'd just let her walk away.

He looked over at the pillow as it sat, lopsided on the sofa. He wanted to go and tear it in two for replacing her but he didn't.

He wanted to smash that cup and the rest of the apartment with it but he didn't. He wanted to set the world on fire for taking her from him, but he didn't. What he did was cry until his heart was wrung dry.

When he was emptied of tears, he opened the cupboard gently and pulled out her mug, placing it carefully on the side so he could see it. Then walked to the sofa and carefully picked up the pillow and replaced it against the wall where it now belonged. And then finally, at a loss to what else to do, he went to bed.

He'd hoped that hiding away from the world would make the pain go away but instead all it did was place him in the same bed they'd shared, where he could still smell her perfume. The pillow she'd slept on next to his, still had a depression in it, where she'd rested her head, so he pulled it to him and held it like he'd held her only that morning.

The glass of water she'd taken to bed the night before, still sat half drunk on the nightstand on her side of the bed. Everything everywhere reminded him of her. It was as if she was infused into his life now for eternity.

His phone vibrated, and he picked it up to see it was a message from Laura.

Laura: Just boarding. This is hard. Msg you in 8 hours. I love you. X

He replied and it broke his heart that they weren't flying home together, sitting next to each other, stealing one another's travel snacks and watching in-flight movies together.

For hours he lay in the growing darkness and thought about her, remembering moments from their time together. Sleep evaded him so he just lay there, hardly moving hour after hour.

The colours had seemingly drained from the world as she'd flown away and everything around him was left in lifeless monochrome. He wanted his colours and his Laura back.

By the time the sun came up, Dan had hardly slept, save for an hour or so just before dawn, brought on by exhaustion rather than a state of peace. Picking up his phone to check on her progress, he saw she'd messaged him while he'd slept to say she was home. Relieved she was safely home, he placed the phone on his chest as he laid back against the headboard and held his arm over his eyes as he tried to adjust to a life without her waking up beside him. He desperately wanted to look at the empty space next to him and instead see her delicious, naked curves crying out to be kissed as she tangled herself up in the bedsheets like she was swimming in a sea of white cotton.

But he knew she wasn't there so he didn't uncover his eyes. She was gone and he knew it. In that moment it became clear to him what he needed to do.

He picked his phone up off his chest and typed.

"Maxxy? Can I speak to mum?"

Chapter 35

The Future

Laura looked glumly into her Prosecco, with Buddy at her feet, wishing she was anywhere but in her parent's living room. It was 11:30 pm and she was relishing getting to bed as soon as it was January 1st. In keeping with the tradition, as it had always been, it was the Grays' year to host festivities, with the families alternating each year. The only significant difference this year was the absence of Dan. And it hurt her more than anyone could imagine.

His sister Issy, had been great, however, spending the earlier parts of the day with Laura, helping tidy up and starting to prep the oversized buffet which without fail each year, threatened to sink whichever dining table it was placed onto.

"Is he calling today?"

Laura knew full well what Dan's sister was getting at; everyone in both families seemed to know that things were happening between the pair without it being explicitly said.

"Yeah, I think so. He has done for the last few days since I got home anyway."

Dan's sister knew that they'd gotten caught up in feelings

and that this New Year would be particularly tough for Laura as he wouldn't be here. It pained her to see the younger woman struggle.

"So you had a nice time then? Over there?" Issy had already heard her brother's side of the story so knew what Laura would likely say, but she still was curious.

"It was wonderful, Issy. If I could have stayed, I would have done. We spent four days just the two of us in our own little world and it was beyond perfect. But now it feels like we're even more apart than ever before." Tears simmered on the surface as she spoke.

"Ah Laura, it'll be okay. You'll see. I spoke to him on Boxing Day. He knows now that you're the one. Come the summer, you two will be back to running around after each other like you used to do as kids, and everything will feel right with the world. When it comes to you two, it's just inevitable."

Laura smiled and hoped that was true but right now as she sat there, longing for the man of her dreams who was three thousand miles away, she felt like it was a lifetime away.

She messaged with him throughout the day as had become their way but nothing she did seemed to lift her spirits. Dan had promised her a video call just before midnight in London, so they could see each other as the celebrations started.

The day had dragged on and on.

Come the evening, Laura just wanted it to be over. She missed him and could not quite shake the glum feeling she had. Even Buddy had got the memo and spent the entire day by her side, her constant companion.

As midnight neared, her Border Collie started to whine, looking towards the window.

"What's up, boy? Have the fireworks started?" Laura knew he was usually pretty good this time of year with all the commotion so it was odd for him to be concerned now. Hearing the front door open and close, Laura looked around the room. *Everyone was here so who was that?* Dave and Brian looked knowingly at her from their seats at one end of the buffet table, Max was trying not to giggle, and even her own mother smiled at her. But none of it made any sense.

Buddy rose from where he was stationed at her feet and padded gently out into the hallway to investigate.

"Laura, did the door just go? Go check and I'll top up your drink." Issy had a certain look on her face that didn't register with Laura at the time, but looking back the morning after it all would make perfect sense.

She felt like she wasn't party to an in-joke and it confused her but she stood up anyway and went into the hall following Buddy, unsure of what she'd find but feeling compelled to go.

"You okay? We good?"

Those four words from that soft deep voice stopped her in her tracks. In front of her, knelt Dan, who was playing with a very happy Border Collie at the front door.

"You came home!"

"I came home."

She rushed into his arms as he stood to greet her and hung on, desperately hoping she hadn't nodded off in front of the TV before midnight, and this wasn't some sick twisted dream her subconscious was making her experience.

But he felt real. He felt here. He felt like he did the last time

263

he held her a few days ago.

Pulling herself free from his embrace Laura needed to understand. "Dan, I don't understand. Why are you here?"

This was the moment Dan had been playing over and over in his head for at least the last few days. An eight-hour flight, trying to decide what to say and how to say it, knowing he'd probably never remember half of what he'd decided. By the time he touched down in Heathrow, he'd made up his mind to just speak from the heart and then all that was left to do was wait it out until it was time.

"I came home. I don't want to be without you any longer; it's just too hard."

On the drive over from his hideout at his parent's house, where he'd waited for the perfect moment since getting back into the country, this was what he'd assumed would be the hard bit, but as he spoke he knew no words would ever be easier to say.

"When you left, I felt like I'd lost half of me; I wasn't expecting it to feel like that. There was a hole where there had been a you. The apartment felt foreign without you in it even though you'd only been there for a few days, but I couldn't stand it; I've not been able to sleep really since you left. I knew by the end of the first night I just needed to come home to you. You're my home, Laura. You're where I want to be.

You're the reason my heart bleeds when you're not around. I want to spend every hour of every day making you happy, no matter what that takes and at what cost to me. I don't ever want to be apart from you again.

So I spoke to my boss and explained my situation and that I couldn't stay. They agreed to let me work the months' notice of my contract remotely and then put me on the next available plane home they could."

Holding her hand gently as he spoke, he lovingly rubbed his thumb over the soft skin on the back of her hand. "I love you, Laura."

She could feel him trembling as he spoke. He was home. For good. He had passed up his dream job to be with her so they could be together. He'd given it all up for her because he was completely and hopelessly in love with her. She could see it written plainly on his beautiful face.

"Dan." She spoke slowly with a half-smile on her face.

"Yeah?"

"You had me at *I came home.* Shut up and kiss me"

With that Dan brought his hands up to cup the side of her face gently and kissed her. It was a kiss for the ages and the world seemed to spin around them as they lost themselves to it; everything outside of the six inch space immediately around them became a blur of light and sound.

"Well fuck me!"

"Brian!" Molly never approved of her husband's swearing.

"What?"

"Pay up, mate," Dave said, holding out his hand in jest.

"Oh, you two and that silly bet." Emily and Molly smiled at each other, rolling their eyes at their respective other halves.

"Ah it's fine, Emily, fair is fair. Dave won."

"Erm, guys? As happy as we are that you're okay with this," Dan gestured towards his embrace with a teary, smiley Laura. "Care to enlighten us as to what the hell is going on?"

Molly Muir walked over to her son and the beautiful Laura and kissed them both on the cheek. "Oh, your dad had a bet with Dave that you'd eventually both get your acts together before they both hit retirement age."

"What?! Since when?"

"New Year's Eve, the first year Laura was at uni. There was just something between you two that night that we felt was inevitable. Don't you remember you spent almost the entire evening in the kitchen together? We all thought you might have gotten together then." Dan's mum had a twinkle in her eye as she hugged Laura.

"I thought you'd get together *after* we both retired." Dave playfully slapped his friend on the shoulder, as Brian Muir put a five-pound note into his friend's hand and smiled.

"Wait a minute." Laura was more taken aback by this than by Dan arriving moments ago. "You all thought this was going to happen?"

"Oh honey, we've always known it was likely to happen one day. There's something that sparks when the pair of you are together."

"And you never thought to mention it to us?" Dan was shaking his head in disbelief, with his hand on Laura's hip desperately not wanting to lose her again, as she hugged his mum.

"Little brother, where's the fun in that? Why do you think Dad suggested Laura came to visit before Christmas? For shits and giggles? Right! Anyway, take these," Issy handed them both a glass of champagne. "There's two minutes until the clock strikes midnight. Time to finally see the New Year in as one big family."

As they all entered the Grays' family living room where Martin and Max were sitting waiting, Dan knew there was one last thing he needed to say. Walking in front of his sister Issy, he felt her push something into his free hand.

"Uncle Dan, if you and Aunty Laura are boyfriend and girlfriend now, does that mean you're going to get married like Mum and Dad?"

"Jesus, Max! Shut up, mate!" Martin sank low into his chair.

"What? What did I say?" His son smirked, knowing exactly what he'd said.

"Hey. Can I ask you something?" He pulled back gently on Laura's hand, stopping her from sitting down as he gave his nephew a wink.

"Of course. You okay? We good?"

"I'm always good when I'm with you, Laura and I want it always to be like that."

"What do you mean?" Laura's head tilted slightly to the left as she asked.

Dan gently lowered himself to one knee and brought forward his free hand which held the small blue box, given to him by Issy just a moment before. *Holy shit he's going to ask me to marry him!*

"Laura, will you marry me and be my past, present and future?"

*

The fireworks began erupting on the street outside as silence held fast in the living room of Dave and Emily Gray, everyone holding their breath, waiting for Laura to speak. The only noise in the room was Buddy panting with excitement.

She didn't need thinking time. She knew her answer. She was just trying to commit this moment to memory; it was perfect beyond measure.

Nodding and crying and smiling and laughing she gave the answer Dan had hoped she'd give.

"Yes!"

Dedicated to all the Lauras who were loved but never knew.

Epilogue

"You okay? We good?" He asked.

She nodded, tears welling in her eyes as she held his hand.

"Love is a beautiful thing. When people use the word love, it's usually associated with playfulness, kisses in the rain and summers that never end. Love is also fighting for what you believe in and being able to say the hard things at the right time to the person you share your life with. Love is being able to say sorry and mean it, forgetting all the things that went before it.

It's holding hands in the dark when you're both scared. It's not always knowing the right words to say but knowing that your presence is what matters the most. True love is for always because that person who completes your heart, is your home and you are theirs.

You're the home I come back to. You always will be."

He took a deep breath and smiled at her.

"You okay? We good?" She asked, through her tears with him looking back at her.

He nodded, watching her scrunching her nose up, trying to find the words.

"When I think about you, I think about how different my life would be without you. If you weren't in my life, everything would be drab and monochrome. You colour my life and my world in ways I never knew were even possible. You have been my friend, my protector and my biggest fan all of my life and I can't imagine ever not being with you.

I want to always hold your hand and face the future together with you. You're the pieces of my puzzle that I can't complete by myself.

I know I'm not as good with words as you are but I know that you know my heart is true; it's yours forever and it always has been."

Tears ran down her face as he gently stroked his thumb over the back of her hand.

"Dan, do you take this woman to be your lawfully wedded wife?"

"I might."

"He does."

"I do."

"Laura, do you take this man to be your lawfully wedded husband?"

"I might."

"She does."

"I do."

The vicar smiled at the pair in front of her, very much in love. "Then by the power vested in me, I now pronounce you husband and wife. Dan, you may kiss the bride."

About the Author

Eliza Hope Brown, born in rural Wiltshire, is a full-time writer of contemporary fiction. She studied English and Foreign Languages at DeMonfort University and was a primary school teacher and graphic designer before writing her first novel in late 2022. She lives in London with her cat, Morley.

Also by Eliza Hope-Brown

Sanctuary

A broken heart, a photographer fixated on his work and a chance meeting in an airport at 4am.

Laura, professional rugby player, strong body, shattered heart, unable to see an end to the pain caused by her former fiancè.

Dan, married to his job and haunted by an image from the past that he just can't shake.

A story that spans years and cities. Crossed paths and kept promises - does coffee really fix everything?

Find sanctuary in a book you won't want to put down.

Printed in Great Britain
by Amazon

23161575R00159